Steady, damn it!" he screamed at the helmsman. The pilot's knuckles were white against the wheel as he fought to keep the ship away from the shore. Jabarra threw the man aside and grabbed the tiller. This stretch of shoreline had claimed countless lives. Known for its rough seas and unpredictable storms, many an admiral lost his life and that of his crew to its jagged labyrinth of stone. Skeletons of uncounted men, some Jabarra once listed among his friends, lay buried beneath the sand. The entire ship shuddered with the tremendous force of the gale. "It'll take more than that to drag me down!" Jabarra screamed into the storm.

**From the creators of the
greatest roleplaying game ever
come tales of heroes, monsters, and magic!**

By T.H. Lain

The Savage Caves

The Living Dead

Oath of Nerull

City of Fire

The Bloody Eye

Treachery's Wake

Plague of Ice
(May 2003)

The Sundered Arms
(July 2003)

Return of the Damned
(October 2003)

The Death Ray
(December 2003)

TREACHERY'S WAKE

T.H. Lain

TREACHERY'S WAKE

Distributed in the United States by Holtzbrinck Publishing.
Distributed in Canada by Fenn Ltd.

Distributed to the hobby, toy, and comic trade in the United States and Canada by regional distributors.

Distributed worldwide by Wizards of the Coast, Inc. and regional distributors.

Cover art by Todd Lockwood and Sam Wood
First Printing: March 2003
Library of Congress Catalog Card Number: 2002113212

9 8 7 6 5 4 3 2 1

US ISBN: 0-7869-2926-X
UK ISBN: 0-7869-2927-8
620-17855-001-EN

U.S., CANADA,
ASIA, PACIFIC, & LATIN AMERICA
Wizards of the Coast, Inc.
P.O. Box 707
Renton, WA 98057-0707
+1-800-324-6496

EUROPEAN HEADQUARTERS
Wizards of the Coast, Belgium
T Hosfveld 6d
1702 Groot-Bijgaarden
Belgium
+322 467 3360

Visit our web site at **www.wizards.com**

Newcoast

A. WAREHOUSES, SHIPPING OFFICES
B. SHANTYTOWN
C. THIEVES' GUILD
D. WEALTHY MERCHANTS HOMES

SEA

SEA

CLIFF

CLIFF

WHARVES

N

Prologue . . . Howling winds whipped through the rigging of the merchant ship. Boiling swells tossed the vessel from side to side as each new wave threatened to send it hurtling into the rocks. The mast groaned against the force of the gale. The edges of the sails snapped in the wind.

It was a large ship by most standards, a cargo runner, one of many that sailed the coast. In the depths of the hull, an ornate box broke from its bindings and slid across the hold. It was long and slender with spidery silver script covering it on all sides — the type of container usually reserved for magical goods.

"Step to," Captain Jabarra bellowed to his men as they wrestled with whipping lines to pull down the mainsheet. "Look alive, or ye won't be much longer!"

Jabarra's name was known all up and down the Fell Coast. Stern but fair treatment ensured that he employed only the finest sailors. A reputation for generous pay rewarded him with a fiercely loyal crew. An uncanny knack for finding the most lucrative cargo made him a wealthy man. His habit of not asking questions didn't hurt.

Jabarra wasn't nearly as interested in where the box came from as in where he needed to take it. The gold he was paid to get it to Newcoast was as good as any in the captain's eyes.

"Steady, damn it!" he screamed at the helmsman.

The pilot's knuckles were white against the wheel as he fought to keep the ship away from the shore. Jabarra threw the man aside and grabbed the tiller. This stretch of shoreline had claimed countless lives. Known for its rough seas and unpredictable storms, many an admiral lost his life and that of his crew to its jagged labyrinth of stone. Skeletons of uncounted men, some Jabarra once listed among his friends, lay buried beneath the sand. The entire ship shuddered with the tremendous force of the gale.

"It'll take more than that to drag me down!" Jabarra screamed into the storm.

On a bluff above the drama, Yauktul watched Gretsch and Murgle lovingly heft a boulder. Gretsch cradled the stone in his right arm as Murgle patted its granite surface. Wind lashed the creature's hide clothing, cutting the stench of its crusted and flaky flesh. Yauktul, his own skin covered with mottled and matted fur, was thankful for the respite from the ettin's putrid smell.

The sudden storm made the gnoll commander's job easier. The boulder would be a delicious flourish to the ship's already savory demise. Yauktul toyed with the idea of letting nature do his work for him, but he thought better of it. It never paid to anger an ettin. He nodded to the foul giant.

With a howl, the ettin hurled the huge rock. It hurtled toward the ship below, growing smaller and smaller before striking with a deep thud, barely audible above the howling storm.

The next morning, as the tide rolled out it uncovered a clutter of smashed timber and broken bodies on the beach. Across the back of the hull, the ship's name was still legible. The letters stood as tall as a man and were painted in flowing script by a skilled hand: *Treachery*.

Red light from the fading sun brought a tinge of pink to the blanket of snow covering the streets of Newcoast. Shopkeepers throughout the market district fastened doors and shutters against the threatening sky, darkening as it was with the hint of strong evening winds and another heavy snow.

Winter hit the Fell Coast with a vengeance, its storms wheeling in on the heels of shortening days. Temperatures began dropping shortly after the season's harvest was reaped and the snows came shortly after. Throughout the region, farmers drug out their brightly colored tents and dusted them off in preparation for a lively harvest festival, yet even the cheer of the midwinter solstice celebration brought only temporary respite from the bitter cold. There was barely enough time to collect the harvest and hastily celebrate its richness by the time the first flakes fell. Soon the entire region sat under a coverlet of white.

In the city's market square, hermits and merchants alike bundled their wares for the trip back to hovel or home. Carts piled high with goods trundled down the narrow city streets, led by mule teams all too eager to escape the chill air. Young aristocrats wrapped in thick fur cloaks hustled off to the warmth and comfort of well-appointed homes, or to indulge themselves in the illicit pleasures of the wharf district. All of the city's inhabitants moved as though with a singular purpose—shelter.

All, that is, save one.

A slight figure slid unnoticed amidst the bustling denizens of Newcoast. Dressed in a modest leather tunic and shrouded in a cloak of dull gray, the halfling woman passed unseen through the tides of humanity washing back and forth across the lively streets. She padded softly through powdery snow, deft feet leaving hardly a print to signal her passing. Habit led the woman along lesser-traveled streets and alleyways.

Standing a few feet shorter than the other major races of the land, the halfling woman was a lean and muscled creature. The hood of her cloak was pulled up over her head, hiding fine features and curled, flowing hair. Supple leather boots clad her small feet, their soles thick enough to keep out the cold and damp of the snowy ground but thin enough to act almost as a second skin and to ensure footing on any terrain. A small crossbow was slung over her shoulder on a leather strap. The weapon's stock rested firmly on the center of her back. A number of small daggers and knives were strapped to her thigh and down the front of her leather armor, safely hidden from prying eyes.

The woman paused beside a cluster of barrels stacked in the alley. She ran a hand along the rough-cut boards of the building's siding, crouching down to rest her legs and catch her breath, taking a minute to watch the people go by and to gauge the crowd.

The city of Newcoast was a bustling metropolis by Fell Coast standards. It profited well from its location as a major hub for ships from the continent of Auralis to the north. Its nobles laid a complex code of taxes and tariffs on every good that passed through the region on its way to kingdoms beyond. Swords and armor from dwarven lands to the south lay crated and waiting along with rare herbs and spices from the barbarian tribes to the west. Candles and soaps, furs and fine linens, dried foodstuffs and rare meats frozen in states of magically induced stasis, all passed through its port.

The seaport's human cargo was no less diverse and interesting. Merchants of all make and description filled the streets of the wharf district by day, haggling and cajoling over prices or attempting to track down lost shipments. Throngs of young boys ran about the docks looking for dropped coins or harassing swarthy captains for work. Drunken sailors reeled down the streets by day and kept the city guard busy with their antics by night. Fist fights erupted as a matter of routine and more than a few enterprising souls made comfortable livings taking bets on the altercations, both spontaneous and planned.

Crouched in the alleyway, the halfling, Lidda, took it all in, reveling in the sights and sounds. She felt quite at home among the seafaring scum.

An elaborately dressed man caught Lidda's eye. He was wrapped in a fur-lined, scarlet cloak, and his boots appeared to be made of fine leather. His stomach hung over the belt at his waist in thick folds of skin in a way that set him apart from the gaunt beggars that he waved aside as he trundled down the street. A few wisps of gray hair fluttered atop his otherwise bald skull. People scattered before him, but the man still used his ledger book like a shield to clear a path for himself.

Lidda waited as the man passed by. She was looking for an opening in the crowd where she might melt into the throng unobserved. A horse-drawn carriage rolling down the street offered her the diversion she sought. On the streets of Newcoast at the close of the business day with a storm on the horizon, it was every peasant for himself. Obviously the wagon driver took that credo to heart. People on the street moved aside as the wagon rumbled past, pressing themselves against buildings and spilling into alleys. The banker shook his fist at the teamsters and muttered under his breath, but he joined the crowd leaping out of the way.

Lidda darted from behind the stack of barrels and fell into step a few paces behind the man. She noted the girth of the rope belt holding his cloak shut as she slid a dagger from a sheath at her thigh. A quick flick of the wrist severed the strap and the follow-through slipped a small slit in the crimson robe. With a spring, Lidda hurled herself into the banker's bulk. Her shoulder hit his back and her hand shot through the slit in his robe.

"Sorry," she muttered, pushing against the man with her arm as though to regain her footing. "You really should be more careful."

Lidda slipped through the press of people and into the alleyway from which she came. A pouch of coins dangled from her hand. She chuckled to herself and dissolved into the crowd on the other side of the alley, well out of sight of her victim. A yell went up from the street behind her, but the rogue was long gone. She dropped the coins into a pocket of her tunic and hurried down the road.

She did, after all, have more important business to attend to.

The thieves' guild in Newcoast occupied a large and elaborately decorated stone building on the outskirts of the city's market district. Erected by a wealthy merchant almost a hundred years previous, the structure functioned as his home and place of business for the first fifty years of its life. It had since become the headquarters of one of the most powerful thieves' guilds on the coast, though it kept the appearance of its former purpose. To most, it was just one of many warehouses sheltering trade goods.

The previous owner had been an entrepreneur of sorts who profited handily in the early days of the first dwarven war against the trolls. His luck eventually ended and a series of poor business decisions ran him afoul of the guild's founding members. The man handed over the building's title to settle an unpaid gambling debt in exchange for keeping nine fingers. It was, the guild masters would say, a mutually beneficial arrangement.

Very few were privy to the "unofficial" business that took place behind the guild's walls. The building did function as a warehouse and clearing house, but most of the goods that passed through the building were stolen. A handful of the city's politicians were in league with the guild and utilized the guild's services when elections drew near, taking credit for city streets largely clean of petty cutpurses and pickpockets.

Lidda approached the door of the guild. The portal stood nearly nine feet tall and was banded with thick pieces of iron. The ornate carvings of the building's previous occupant had been sanded smooth and the door was quite simple. She patted the pouch of coins in her tunic and knocked. A small, square section of wood slid open in the center of the door a few feet above Lidda's head. A moment later, it snapped shut again and a similar door, this time at the halfling woman's eye level, slid open.

"Name and business, please," a stern voice prompted from behind the hole.

"Name's Lidda," she replied. "I have dealings with Eva Flint."

"Yes, m'lady was expecting you an hour ago. You're running a touch late, eh?"

"Some other pressing business came up," the halfling replied, "so if you'd be so kind as to open up . . ."

Lidda heard the intricate working of a number of locks and bolts and the groan of wood on wood as the door swung inward. She stepped inside.

The guild's interior was as impressive and imposing as its outside. Heavy, well-worked stone blocks betrayed the building's dwarven origins, each stone fitting its neighbor precisely. Dim lighting from sparsely placed wall sconces added to the guild's ominous feel and Lidda's sense that her every move was being scrutinized by an unseen watcher, no doubt peering at her through a tiny spy hole. The doorkeeper, a severe looking man, short and lean of stature, cleared his throat.

"Follow me, please," he said, his voice still hushed but with an urgent undertone. "Watch the third brick on the right there," he said, pointing to a section of flooring, "it's a bit loose."

Lidda gave the stone a wide berth as she walked past. What sort of trap the stone triggered she could only guess at. That it was trapped went without saying in Lidda's mind. Providing they managed to avoid prison or death, most rogues would eventually find themselves in the patronage of a guild. Until that happened, underground networks of thieves could be just as dangerous to a fledgling pickpocket as the authorities. Jail cells or a stab in the back aside, Lidda knew that she would be contacted sooner or later.

For her, sooner had been just a few days ago.

Eva Flint's room was larger and more impressively decorated than most in the guild. The guild master was seated behind a great oak desk, leafing through a leather-bound ledger. A single candle and a small pot of ink were the desk's only adornment. Eva closed the ledger as Lidda was shown into the room. The light from the candle added a highlight of yellow to the woman's short, red hair. The short sleeves of her loose-fitting blouse showed off well-defined muscles. Were she not seated, Eva would have towered above Lidda's head. Her face was stern and chiseled but not unattractive.

"You're late," Eva said sharply, pushing her chair back on its two rear legs and kicking her feet up onto the desk.

"Yes, I'm sorry, m'lady," Lidda said, stepping forward and drawing the pouch of coins from inside her tunic. She dropped the sack on the desk, where it landed with the pleasing jingle of coin on coin. "I would have been here earlier, but I was caught up with some other business that I thought you might appreciate."

"Well, at least I see that you have respect for guild protocol, even if your sense of time is a bit off. That banker that you 'did business' with is a regular customer of the guild who's fallen behind on his bills. You've just saved me an unpleasant house call." An upward curl tugged at the corners of Eva's mouth, taking the edge from her words as she looked Lidda up and down. "This might work out yet."

So, Lidda realized, she had been followed that day and quite possibly for many days previous. It made sense—the guild contacted her, not vice-versa. Still, she was unsettled at the prospect of having been on the rodent's end of a cat and mouse game. It was a situation the rogue was not used to and definitely not fond of.

"I'm glad that you accepted my offer of meeting," Eva continued. "I'd hate to have to drive you from town, or worse. I think that you will find an association with the guild quite advantageous."

Eva rose and moved to a door on the side of the room. She opened the door and an elderly man entered. He wore a long blue robe laced with intricately embroidered patterns of silver thread. He was clearly of the magic using sort. Judging by the deep wrinkles lining his face, he had attained great age, and Lidda knew that where wizards were concerned, great age and great power often went hand in hand.

"Allow me to introduce Horace Wotherwill," Eva said as the man moved through the door.

Wotherwill stepped forward and took Lidda's hand in his own. His dry and wrinkled skin reminded Lidda of a goblin's hide in its roughness and she had to fight back the urge to pull her hand from his.

"Pleased to meet me, I'm sure," Wotherwill said, "but let's drop the pleasantries for now. We have important business."

2

"I will not go!"

Krusk's meaty fist came down hard on the table, sending a cascade of dark ale sloshing over the side of his earthenware mug and turning heads among the evening's patrons of the Bung and Blade. Even in the midst of such a motley crew as was gathered at the pub, there were none interested in meeting the eyes of a pair of arguing half-orcs. Glances quickly shifted back to plates of food.

Malthooz drew back from the table. Though three years older and nearly his physical equal, Malthooz was in every other way Krusk's opposite. His eyes ran along the steel studs embedded in the tough leather of Krusk's shoulder armor then trailed down to the cruel dagger that was bound to his forearm in a makeshift scabbard of thick hide straps. He glanced at the massive axe resting against Krusk's chair, then down at his own humble rucksack, stuffed as it was with books. He looked up as Krusk hid his frown behind his mug.

They were both hulks by human standards, but Krusk was large even for a half-orc. Lean and corded muscles ran the length of his body, honed over years of rough living and many fights. His face was scarred in a few places, the most cruel running from just under his left earlobe to his jaw. It was a trophy from a brawl with an ogre that had almost cost Krusk his life but earned him a double-headed magical axe instead.

Malthooz was not nearly so bulky. He could still best almost any man in an arm wrestling match by sheer strength, but he was clumsy and untested in the realm of combat. From the time they were children, he was drawn more to books than swords. Malthooz was often the butt end of the other barbarian children's jokes and pranks. He felt the sting of cruelty even more acutely for the rift that had grown between he and Krusk over the intervening years.

Both men had the pale, gray-greenish skin of a half-orc and a tell-tale protrusion of teeth from their lower jaw. Wiry, black hair sprouted from their skin in odd patches. They were rough looking but not ugly. By nonhuman standards, they might even be considered handsome. Among humans, half-orcs were sometimes tolerated but seldom truly welcomed. Krusk and Malthooz, unrelated in any way but race, had both found a home within a village of outcasts. It was there, amidst the mixed population of humans, elves, dwarves, and half-breeds, that their shared heritage created a bond that approximated family.

Malthooz sighed and said, "This autumn has been hard on the village. The dire wolves have returned in greater numbers. Game is becoming scarce. Our people are disheartened." He paused. "I don't know that our chief will live to see the spring. The village needs your strength, Krusk."

Krusk lowered his eyes as his mug sank slowly toward the table. If he was startled by the news, it did not register on his face.

"The village is of no concern to me now," Krusk snorted, meeting Malthooz's gaze. "When I left there, I vowed never

to return. It was my home for a short time, but their ways—
our ways — are not mine. I could never follow your way of
life and wither away in that frozen wasteland that you call
a home."

"Look around you," Malthooz urged. "Are you so at home
here, so keen to grasp for the favor of a society that has no
place for you?"

Malthooz looked about the pub's dim and smoky interior.
All around himself he saw the truth of his words. Cutthroats
and ruffians of all stripes patronized the Bung and Blade,
ever eager to pick the pockets of those who overindulged
in the tavern's strong and bitter brew or to slit a throat in the
back alley of anyone who's purse looked worth the trouble.
If a person wanted trouble, he need look no farther than the
pub.

"Look around," Malthooz repeated. "We are outcasts among
even these outcasts. No other place in town would let us in the
door."

"At least I know my place among these people," Krusk said,
"and am free to do as I please." He downed the last of his ale,
banging the mug hard on the table to alert the barmaid that
he was ready for another. "The villagers live in fear. They could
never understand my need for freedom. You should not have
come here."

Malthooz looked up as the door of the pub swung open and
two figures entered the room. A flurry of snowflakes followed
them in on the evening breeze. They were bundled against the
chill, the fringes of their woolen cloaks white with frost.

Malthooz watched as the first woman entered. Shocks of
long, black hair spilled from her fur-lined hood, and the light
tan of a leather collar showed just above the neckline of her
cloak. She tossed the hood back and her hair cascaded down
the sides of her slender face. Small, pointed ears jutted from
behind long ringlets of ebony. She gripped a slim staff of

wood in one hand, its silver-crusted top standing just above her head. The staff and the large, leather pouch slung over her shoulder marked the woman as a wizard just as her pointed ears marked her as an elf. She was willowy thin but not fragile looking.

Malthooz instantly recognized the woman's high-elf ancestry. While most humans had little power to discern between the elf races aside from their often outlandish differences in dress and custom, Mialee's fine, white skin and simple but elegant features set her apart from any but the most beautiful of wood or wild elves.

A druid entered next. She stood slightly taller than the wizard and looked a bit wilder. She shared her companion's elf features, but Malthooz thought she lacked the other's refined look and air of grace. A small rack of antlers was rolled up into the front of her stark, white hair and her cloak lacked the civilized look of the wizard's. Feathers were woven into the long braids that fell from her temples. Malthooz noted the jeweled hilt of a scimitar sticking out of the front of her forest green tunic. Though not a pureblooded wild elf, he thought, the lines of high and wild were crossed somewhere in the woman's past.

Malthooz watched the druid scan the pub's interior. She took in her surroundings as a deer might scan the forest for predators before kneeling for a drink. With a nod to her companion, the two started across the floor. The druid's hand slipped over the hilt of her sword. The wizard looked unconcerned. The women approached the table where Malthooz and Krusk sat.

"Is this a new trend?" the wizard asked, seating herself next to Krusk. "I didn't know that you actually had any friends." She grinned at Malthooz. "From the looks of this one, he's not here to help us ambush wealthy merchants or disembowel pesky beasts."

Malthooz's cheeks reddened as he cast his eyes down to the table with a self-conscious chuckle. Krusk shot Mialee a cruel stare.

"This is Malthooz, the one I told you about," he grunted. "He wants me to return to his home with him."

The wizard stuck out her hand and said, "The name's Mialee—pleased to meet you."

Malthooz took her hand awkwardly.

"And this is Vadania," she said, tossing her head back in the druid's direction. "She doesn't say much."

Vadania nodded a greeting.

"So you're the one who wants to take our Krusk away?" Mialee asked.

Malthooz felt the woman sizing him up with her eyes. A barmaid came by the table and plunked a new mug of ale in front of Krusk.

"An ale for me and another for the brute here, and—" Mialee raised an eyebrow at Malthooz and he nodded—"one for him as well," she said, reaching for the sack of silver coins hanging on her belt. "Food for us all, and a pot of steaming water and an empty mug for the druid." Mialee dropped a few silver coins onto the barmaid's serving tray, then turned back to Malthooz. "So why would you want to take our Krusk away?"

"My people more than I, elf." Malthooz began. "The lure of gold and tales of adventure have taken their toll on my village. The youth are no longer content with the old ways. Those of us who stay pay the price for this wanderlust. We can't keep up with the wolves and the worgs. Stories coming from the north of goblin raids are getting more and more worrisome."

The barmaid returned with a tray of mugs and four bowls of stew. She set one in front of each of the companions and placed a pot of steaming water before Vadania. Malthooz watched with interest as the druid drew a pouch of herbs from her pack. She dumped the pungent mixture of dried leaves into the pot. As she bent down to return the pouch to her pack, Vadania's foot caught the edge of Malthooz's pack. The bag went over on its side, spilling a pile of books and a wooden disk on the floor.

Vadania's eyes widened and she asked, "You cast, half-orc?"

Malthooz hastily scooped the books back into his pack and drew the drawstrings tight.

"No," he said curtly, shoving the pack farther under his seat. "They're nothing. Just . . ." he stumbled for words, "some reading."

Vadania shrugged and said. "Your secrets are your own, half-orc."

She took a sip of the strong-smelling brew. Malthooz glanced at Krusk, but he appeared to have noticed nothing.

"I know difficulty better than most," Vadania said. "My people have also felt the sting of rebelliousness in our younger folk." She set her mug on the table. "And I am one of them. I cannot answer for the problems of my entire race. I do what I do."

"Besides," Mialee cut in, "Krusk has already said he's sticking with us. Right?"

The wizard stuck the barbarian in the side with a bony elbow. Krusk nodded with a grunt.

"So, enough of this," Mialee said. "Besides, Lidda will be here soon and we can find out what she's got for us that's so important."

"Good work, I hope," Krusk grumbled.

Mialee spilled a few silver coins from a pouch onto the table and said, "Any work, I'd say."

Mialee just finished counting the coins for the third time when the door to the pub swung open and Lidda walked through. The halfling pushed her way to their table at the rear of the pub and took the remaining empty seat next to Vadania.

"I'm glad all of you made it," Lidda said, pausing as she

looked pointedly at the unfamiliar half-orc seated with her companions. "All of you and then some."

Mialee jumped in, saying in a low growl that almost approximated Krusk's voice, "Lidda, this is Malthooz. Malthooz, meet Lidda."

"He wants to take Krusk back north," Vadania offered. "Long story, it can wait."

"Yes, it can," Krusk growled. "Why don't we just get to the matter at hand. Do you have a job?"

"Good work, good pay," Lidda said. "An easy job."

She gave Malthooz a sidelong glance. He saw the others straighten at Lidda's words and huddle themselves closer to the woman.

"He's all right, Lidda," Krusk interjected. "He's not much, but he's harmless. If you trust me, you can trust him."

She continued, "It seems a local wizard has been waiting for a shipment that never arrived and he wants to hire a crew to find it for him." She dropped her voice to a whisper and gave each of them a measured look. "He's working through the local guild to keep it hushed."

"No!" Krusk growled. "I'll not work for their like."

Lidda looked around the room to see if anyone was watching or listening.

"Keep it down, you oaf," she said.

Malthooz watched Krusk's hand tighten on his mug. He glanced around the room himself, wondering what he was getting himself into.

"It'll be easy," Lidda said, "and you won't have to deal with the 'likes' of anyone. Leave that to me. Just hear me out."

Krusk growled, but Lidda ignored him.

"A traveling merchant claims that he spotted a recent shipwreck up the coast a few days back. The wizard caught word of this and is convinced that his shipment, some sort of artifact, lies in the wreckage."

"Enough," Krusk said. "I'll hear no more. Wizards, artifact, thieves guilds—I want no part in this."

"You want to pay for breakfast tomorrow?" Mialee asked. "We don't have much choice."

Vadania nodded and said, "And it sounds like a good break for Lidda, if this guild can be trusted."

Lidda grinned.

"I knew you'd have a level head at least, Vadania."

The druid sipped her tea then added, "Besides, Krusk, I know you're probably as eager to get out of this city as I am."

Krusk snorted.

The wind and snow tapered off during the night but not before draping the city beneath a fresh blanket of white. The five companions moved down the empty streets of Newcoast under cover of the predawn darkness. The guards hardly gave the group a second glance as it passed between two tall, wooden towers and beneath the open portcullis of the city's western gatehouse.

The road from the city wound through outlying fields and farms, homesteads that kept the city fed, and fueled much of the trade that occurred inside its walls. At the edge of the horizon to the west, the road disappeared into the forest of Deepwood and eventually made its way to the coast beyond.

They were on their way to meet the wizard Horace Wotherwill. Lidda had arranged the meeting through the guild even before returning to the inn the evening before, a bit of presumption that bothered Krusk more than anyone else. That, and the guild's usual insistence on utter secrecy in this, as in all its dealings. Krusk was convinced that the whole affair would end in serious trouble.

Malthooz walked beside him. Sweat speckled his forehead and his breathing was quick and shallow though they had come only a few miles. Krusk exhaled, each breath a thick huff of steam. His brow was furrowed in disgust, though it wasn't the frigid air that upset him.

"You carry too many books in your pack," Krusk said. "You won't get far with so much worthless paper weighing you down."

Malthooz's reply was flat and emotionless. "I made it as far as Newcoast, I'll make it as far as I need. Why don't you just admit that you don't want me along because my presence reminds you of duties that you'd rather ignore?"

Krusk laughed. "Duties, you say? My only duty now is to protect you — as if looking out for the women was not enough. You shouldn't have come with us."

"Hey," Mialee said, quickening her pace and coming alongside the half-orcs. "Don't give yourself too much credit, Krusk. We ladies can care for ourselves, and I'm sure Malthooz can do the same."

She shot Malthooz a quick wink.

Krusk grunted, "We'll see."

As the morning wore on, the terrain they passed through grew less populated. Family farms dotted the rolling hills. A few lonely souls gathered firewood or tended to pitiful herds, but most were either too busy or too weary to acknowledge the group's passing.

Wotherwill's hut sat on the far boundaries of the city. It was one of the last, scattered, tiny cottages marking the edge of Newcoast's influence. Beyond lay the thick forest of Deepwood. The wizard's shack stood out in odd contrast to the drifted snow piled almost to its windows. It was a squat, stout building made of logs from the nearby woods. A circular window sat on either side of the covered porch in front of the home. Thin curls of smoke rose from the chimney. Heat from the bricks melted snow from the roof, sending a trickle of water down the shingles to form icy spears on the eaves.

After the bustle of the city, Krusk appreciated the dwelling's humble and unpretentious look.

The wizard welcomed the companions into his home. The reek of old leather and the sweet smell of aging parchment, no doubt from the overstuffed bookshelves lining the walls, filled Krusk's nose. A wood-burning stove sat in one corner of the hut's single room. A copper teapot bubbled gently atop it, wafting ribbons of steam. Wotherwill's bed took up another corner, while a desk and chair occupied the last. An oak table dominated the center of the room. Despite its small size, the place looked comfortable enough.

"I'm glad you've come," the wizard said as the companions filed in. "The loss of the artifact has been a grave concern to me and I am eager to have it in my possession."

He sat in a chair at the head of the table and beckoned the others to take a seat. Krusk eyed the rickety furniture.

"It will hold, half-orc. Though it looks to lack physical strength, it has been magically enhanced."

The barbarian sat down and found the chair to be remarkably sound.

Wotherwill continued, "I've worked with Lady Flint before and trust her judgment." He turned to Lidda. "I understand this will be your first assignment for the guild?"

The rogue nodded.

"Eva told me she's had her eye on you for some time. She thinks you can be trusted." He looked over each of the companions in turn, pausing to stare at Malthooz a bit longer than the others. "You seem out of place, half-orc. I don't remember Eva mentioning a pair of you?"

"He's with us," Krusk jumped in. "He's all right."

Lidda nodded.

"So be it." The wizard took a sip of his tea before continuing, "The staff you seek is of timeless design and ancient power. Many foolhardy warriors have lost their lives trying to claim it for their own. Myself, I have devoted a goodly portion of my life to its recovery. Just last autumn my work came to fruition.

"Two centuries ago, a baron named Vernon Ghaldarous stole a powerful staff from a traveling mage. Ghaldarous' goons sneaked into the man's tent as he slept and slit his throat. They took the staff and tossed his body into the bay. Unfortunately for the baron, the mage placed a curse upon the staff that would turn its magic back upon itself in anyone's hands but his own. The power to influence and befriend even the most stubborn of people turned the baron's allies against him and his enemies into allies. He found himself attracting the most unappealing friends as the power of the staff altered and changed. Evil and deceit soon surrounded him. Life became a cruel game of survival as his new acquaintances coveted the staff for themselves. Attempts on his life became a daily occurrence. Eventually he fled into the icy wastes of northern Auralis and disappeared.

"Over the years, many have sought the staff for their own, both with hopes of raising armies of evil and hopes of restoring the cursed item to its previous state. Until recently, no one succeeded in locating the relic." Wotherwill paused for another sip of tea. "I lost my own son to the search when his party was besieged by a band of frost giants. Only two of the original ten survived.

"Two weeks ago, the ship *Treachery* left the town of Umberton in northern Auralis, with the survivors and the staff. It never arrived here and I am convinced that the staff lies within the wreckage."

"Bah," Vadania spat, "there'll be nothing left but swollen timbers by the time we arrive. The coast swarms with bandits and orcs. It's sure to have been looted."

"That might be true, druid, but I'd wager my life that none

of them possesses the key to unlock the wards placed upon the chest that holds the staff."

Wotherwill reached into his tunic and retrieved a slender, silver chain. Dangling from its end was a small, obsidian trinket in the shape of a dragon taking flight. He set the necklace on the table.

Mialee grabbed the thing.

"Strangest key I've ever seen," she said, turning the figurine over in her hand.

"It will open the box that holds the staff," Wotherwill said. "Nothing else in existence will. Its creation was one of the baron's final acts. Whether he hoped to keep the staff from ever doing harm again, or suffered delusions of somehow using it after death, we will never know. His journal gave no clue, but it did lead me to the key."

"And you trust it to us?" Krusk asked, scowling.

"It stays with me, half-orc. Call it insurance against another theft. Or against your failure."

"Why not go yourself?" Lidda asked. "You seem capable enough. Surely if you plan on using the staff you have the magic necessary to see yourself safely to the wreck and back."

"You flatter me, thief, but age is quickly catching up with me. I'd rather save myself for study. That's my interest. I am not so vain as to think that I could use the staff myself."

Wotherwill finished his tea and rose from the table. He took the dragon key and moved to a cupboard on the wall, where he dropped the key into a small chest on the shelf and closed the lid.

"If you return the staff to me, you will be well rewarded for your efforts."

"Now you talk sense," Krusk said, "though I still don't like the sound of this. Why is the thieves guild involved?"

"I'll not risk the task to just any band of adventurers, barbarian. You might understand why I want to keep word of the job quiet. Working with the guild is as strong an assurance of silence as I can get."

Krusk looked around the table. Lidda's face was impossible to read. He knew that she was eager to earn the favor of a guild. He couldn't blame her, but he knew where she stood as a result of her enthusiasm. Malthooz stared at the rows of books on the wall. Vadania, at least, seemed to share his skepticism.

"And you only hope to study?" she asked.

"The item would be discovered eventually. Better that it rest in the hands of one who understands its power than fall into the wrong ones. You of all people should know this, druid."

"What's the guild's cut," Lidda asked, running her fingers along a groove in the tabletop.

"Enough to keep hush," Wotherwill replied. "Yours is enough to ensure that I can find others if you don't want the work." He paused, then added almost as an afterthought, "Though you probably know too much already."

Krusk rose and reached for the handle of his axe.

Wotherwill stepped away from the cupboard, one hand sligthly raised.

"You don't want to go there, friend" he said.

Lidda rose from the table, glaring at Krusk, and said, "We'll take the job."

Krusk shook his head in resignation.

Wotherwill nodded.

"I thought that you would," he said.

The sun was full in the sky by the time the companions collected their gear and said their parting words to the old wizard. The warmth of the sun and the clear blue sky lifted the oppressive feeling of the previous days' storm from the air. They all welcomed the change in weather. Traveling through the snow was one thing, traveling under the specter of a blizzard was quite another.

Deepwood. The name spoke of dark and untold danger. While the edges of the forest provided ample wood for the region's hearths and a bounty of wild game for the hunter, its farther reaches were seen only by the adventurous few. Most travelers gladly accepted the extra days needed to skirt the forest to the north or south. Those for whom time was more pressing recognized the risk as a necessary one. Many did survive their journey through the woods and they bore the scars to prove it. Trolls and brigands were the forest's only true residents.

Vadania took her position at the front of the group. The half-orcs fell in a few steps behind her. Krusk abandoned his large traveling backpack for a smaller shoulder pack. He kept his greataxe slung to his hip, within easy reach. Malthooz still carried his full regimen of books.

Lidda padded along a few dozen yards behind the main group, keeping watch over their backs to ensure they were not taken unawares from behind. Though each of the company kept his weapons within easy reach, if Malthooz's walking staff could be considered such, Lidda's drawn and loaded crossbow was the only one at the ready.

As morning wore into midday, the forest closed in, over, and around them. Arched branches formed a kind of tunnel above the path they traveled, keeping out all but a few rays of sunshine. Thick underbrush crowded the trunks of the trees, which became larger the farther they pressed into the forest.

Lidda watched Malthooz and Krusk exchange a few words. She couldn't hear what they said, but Krusk's tone was enough to let her know that the words weren't pleasant. She moved past the elves and tapped Krusk on the shoulder.

"Why don't you take rear guard for a while?"

Krusk started to protest, but Lidda's look stopped him. He mumbled under his breath and fell to the rear of the group.

"I don't know what his problem is," she said to Malthooz, shaking her head, "but it's not you. He's usually like this."

"He thinks I should never have come looking for him," Malthooz said, "and I suspect he's right."

"No one ever accused him of not being stubborn," Lidda chuckled. "Maybe you should lay off him for a while."

They came upon a clearing late in the day and where they decided to pass the night. Malthooz dropped his pack, sat down on a tangle of roots, and began tugging a boot from his foot. By the time he had the second one off, the others were busy preparing a camp.

From his seat at the edge of the camp, he watched the

company performing like a well-scripted play. Vadania left to hunt for game while Mialee and Lidda gathered wood for a fire. Krusk huddled over a pile of dry moss, flicking sparks from his flint and steel. Malthooz flexed his aching toes self-consciously.

He pulled his boots back on.

"What can I do?" he asked.

Mialee dropped an armful of wood into a growing pile.

"There're game paths all over these woods," she said, tossing a water skin to the half-orc. "There must be a stream or pool around somewhere nearby."

Malthooz nearly fell into the pool before he realized it was there. He'd been wandering, lost in his thoughts. He had no idea how far he'd come from the camp, though the fading light and deepening shadows told him it had been some time. He knelt at the edge of the pond and plunged the empty skin into the water.

As bubbles from the water skin roiled the still, warm water, Malthooz glanced around, paying attention to his surroundings for the first time since leaving the camp. A wall of rock bordered the pool on the far side. A fissure near the center looked like the opening to a cave. The snows, so deep near the city, hadn't fallen as heavily that far into the forest. Only a smattering of white patches showed on the carpet of pine needles. Still, the air was cold, and getting colder as the light faded.

But the water in the pond felt warm, Malthooz realized with a jolt, when it should be icy cold.

A gurgling screech from inside the wall nearly made Malthooz lose his grip on the water skin. A spray of steam followed the shriek. Seconds later, the strangest creature

Malthooz had ever seen flew from the mouth of the cave. It was small, just a few feet tall, he estimated, skinny as a rail, and covered in glistening scales.

The creature tumbled through the air and hit the water in front of Malthooz with a tremendous splash. The half-orc scrambled back from the water's edge, leaving the water skin bobbing in the pond. His foot caught on an exposed root and he flopped clumsily onto his back.

The creature's eyes emerged from the pool—huge, black orbs dripping water. Translucent eyelids blinked away some of the moisture. A frail hand snaked out and tossed the water skin at Malthooz's feet. The arm was covered with folds of blue-green skin that looked like seaweed. Water oozed from the creature's scales.

"This isn't mine, so it must be yours," it said with a burbling voice like gushing water. "Keep your trash out of my pond. Now I've got to defend my home."

With that, it disappeared beneath the water. Malthooz watched the creature's shadowy form swim rapidly back into the cave.

Within moments, a thick, black stink floated from the cave mouth, assailing Malthooz's nostrils and causing him to wretch. A second creature, even more bizarre than the first, drifted from the cave enveloped in a cloud of steam. It landed with a soft plop on the bank of the pool next to the half-orc.

The cloud of vapor rising from the creature obscured its body. Steaming water dripped from its fingers and Malthooz felt heat radiating from it. Its face was dour, a mood accented by the creature's sharp, angular features. It spoke to Malthooz with a voice of vapor that was as easy to see as it was to hear, like the sound of a freshly forged blade being plunged into an ice bath for tempering.

"You'd best leave now," it said. The heat of the creature's

words caused Malthooz to take a step back. "This issue is not your concern."

The half-orc nodded, unable to speak.

"Leave now!" the creature emphasized. The air temperature around it rose noticeably and steam percolated from its pores. It raised a wispy arm as if to strike. "This is my pond and you are not welcome!"

Further speech was cut short by a loud, squishing sound. The creature and its vapor cloud reeled back as a colorful blob of ichor slammed into the side of its head.

Steam poured in a torrent from the creature's nostrils and ears as it turned to face the fish-eyed creature whose head bobbed up and down near the center of the pool. Raising its smoking arms toward the sky, the steam-thing conjured a small cloud of wisps that transformed into a hail of boiling rain. Malthooz scrabbled across the frozen dirt to get away. Sharp points of pain pierced his back as droplets of superheated water pelted him. He howled as the water raised welts along his forearms and the backs of his legs. He tried covering himself with leaves and dirt but could not stop the searing rain.

As suddenly as it began, the torrent stopped. The creature was spent and wheezing, its breath a raspy gurgle of mist.

The fish-eyed creature, apparently unharmed, ducked beneath the surface of the pool.

Vadania was having little luck with her hunt. She knew the forest was full of smaller creatures of all sorts—she saw signs of them all around—but she was unable to locate any. Perhaps something kept them away. She turned back toward camp, resigning herself to a meal of dried rations, when she heard Malthooz's howl.

She found the pool quickly enough. Drawing her scimitar, Vadania stepped into the clearing around the pool and assessed the situation. The half-orc was on the ground near the edge of the pool. A creature—a steam mephit—stood near the fallen half-orc. Another, a water mephit, floated near center of the pond.

The druid extended her free hand toward the steam mephit. Bright yellow-blue flame sprang forth from her upturned palm. The fire crackled with magical intensity as she advanced on the mephit, startling the creature as it caught sight of her in the corner of its eye. Scalding water dripped from the creature's jowls as it backed away from the approaching druid. The steam mephit sprayed torrid mist as it inched away from the advancing elf.

"No haste, elf, it is a misunderstanding," the mephit said as it raised its arms in surrender.

Vadania halted as another ball of ichor smacked the steam mephit in the back of the head. Malthooz grabbed his staff and was on his feet in an instant. He swung the pole in a wide arc that caught the creature in the midsection, doubling it over. Vadania snapped her wrist, sending the flame from her hand to the creature. It hit the mephit's head with a hiss.

The mephit enveloped itself in a cloud of steam and bolted for the pool. The water mephit's laughter sent a ring of waves throughout the pond before it ducked under the surface and disappeared.

Vadania rushed to Malthooz's side, catching him as the pain of his burns overtook him and he crumpled to his knees.

A trail of fog drifted from the surface of the water, marking the steam mephit's retreat.

Vadania helped Malthooz to his feet.

"We need to move," she said. "This is no place to linger."

They started back to camp, Malthooz supporting himself

on the druid's shoulder, and the noise of the quarreling mephits was soon lost in the distance.

It was replaced by another, more ominous sound.

They shuffled through the forest as fast as Malthooz's wounds would allow. Vadania held an arm under the half-orc's shoulder, letting him rest some of his weight on her. The burns on his skin looked to be superficial, but the druid knew that they were probably agonizing to bear and that they were made more so by each step he took. She didn't have time to stop and administer a healing spell.

From somewhere behind her, Vadania heard the underbrush being trampled aside. Whatever was after them was moving through the forest with abandon. She heard branches snapping and could just make out the rhythmic booming of massive footsteps. Whatever she heard, the druid realized it must be huge, considered the spacing between its thumping footsteps. She pushed Malthooz harder as she sensed the sounds gaining on them. She could almost feel the monster's breath on the back of her neck. Vadania glanced back over her shoulder but saw no sign of any pursuer. Twigs brushed her face as they fled, leaving fine traces of blood on her cheeks. She urged Malthooz on, alternately dragging and pushing him. The half-orc's eyes were wide with fear.

Vadania knew the general direction of the camp, but not precisely how far she'd come. Malthooz's call had set her in motion and she'd been too intent on finding the half-orc to notice the distance she'd covered reaching the pool. Her legs burned as she drove them for all their worth.

In the distance, Vadania saw a flicker of fire. She headed straight for the light, dragging the half-orc beside her. Malthooz looked as if he was near the point of passing out. All color was drained from his cheeks and his breath came in ragged gasps. The druid shouted as they neared the circle of the camp, though she was certain the others must have heard the sounds of their crashing approach.

Mialee rushed to Vadania's side as the fleeing pair stumbled into the clearing. She grabbed Malthooz from the druid's grasp and tried ineffectually to support his bulk, but they both spun into the brush on the far side of the camp and collapsed in a tangle of branches.

Krusk was on his feet, moving to the edge of the firelight as the grayish mass of a troll burst through the underbrush on the heels of the druid. He extended his axe in front of himself as the creature rolled over him. One enormous arm swept across the barbarian's side as the troll lumbered past, the knuckles of its other hand dragging along the ground. Krusk doubled over from the impact of the monster's fist slamming into his side and he reeled into the trees.

Lidda grabbed a burning branch from the fire and shoved it into Vadania's hand.

"Take this," she said. "They hate it."

The troll stopped at the sight of the flames and batted at the druid with two bulky hands as it tried to get at her. It moved its misshapen and hunched body awkwardly. Vadania knew that its mortal fear of fire would only discourage the beast for a short time. She held the makeshift torch in front of herself, waving it in the troll's face. The sputtering tip of the branch highlighted the creature's rubbery skin and a putrid, green mass of writhing flesh atop its head. It looked more like folds of leather cord than hair. A long bunch of the stuff dangled in front of the creature's mouth, a cruel approximation of a nose. Stubs of teeth lined it's jaw, worn smooth from gnawing through the bones of its prey, and yellow, syrupy saliva dripped from its chin.

The troll sprang. Vadania dodged to the side and it flew past her. The monster landed on the far side of the camp and spun around. Vadania's shoulders heaved as she tried to catch her breath. Before she could blink, the thing was coming back at her. It covered the ground between them in seconds, moving with a sudden grace that belied its clumsy appearance and its earlier attacks. She dived aside again as the thing came at her, swinging massive, clawed fists.

Krusk used the handle of his weapon to lever himself onto his feet. A quick shake cleared his head and he charged the beast, a yell blasting from his throat. His axe slashed down, severing one of the troll's arms below the elbow. The limb spun to the dirt, but it did not simply lie there. The detached claw scrabbled through the damp leaves of the forest floor, scooting along the ground in a wide arc. The troll swatted Krusk aside and grabbed for its severed body part. The beast held the wriggling limb up to the stump at its elbow. Green blood dripping from the end of the wounded arm bubbled as the missing part touched it. With a sickening, squishing sound, the two halves fused together.

"How can we fight such a being?" Vadania yelled as she rolled to her feet.

She cast the torch aside and drew her scimitar, stepping around to the far side of the fire, keeping the flames between herself and the troll. She wished that she hadn't wasted her own fire spell on the mephit.

Mialee came to the druid's side waving a torch in one hand and sending a barrage of magic missiles into the troll from the tip of the other. The wizard's bolts sizzled through the tough skin of the troll's side.

"We'll never outrun the thing," Mialee gasped.

She whipped the flaming branch around and caught the monster in its side, just below the blackened holes where her magic struck.

The troll lashed out at Mialee with its clublike hands and claws, grabbing at her neck. Mialee ducked under the troll's swing, but saw the thick, razor-sharp nails sail over her head and shred the bark of a nearby tree.

Lidda scampered nimbly between the legs of the troll, hacking at its ankles as she passed. The size of her opponent dwarfed the halfling, making her appear no more than a child. A line of blood marked her weapon's path across the monster's stringy calf.

The four of them surrounded the thing, hacking with a renewed fury, trying to gain an advantage against flesh whose wounds healed before their eyes.

Vadania's stomach churned at the thought of the abomination they faced. It was a vulgar affront to the natural world, a cruel and twisted play on the eternal cycle of death and rebirth. The creature's metabolism was sped up to the point that harm was irrelevant. If that was the case, the druid thought, she must take the battle to the core of the process.

She concentrated her attack on the troll's neck, slashing with the tip of her scimitar at the corded muscles connecting the troll's head to its body. Living flesh closed around her blade, sticking it fast. Fighting against her own revulsion as much as the troll's flailing claws, she dug her weapon into the base of the monster's skull. She hammered the heel of her hand against the hilt of her sword, driving the blade through layers of tissue and bone, probing for the soft brain beneath.

She felt something give and realized it was the sword's tip piercing the back of the cranium. The troll dropped to its knees. Its arms still flailed, but without conscious control, only reflex. Vadania jumped back, leaving her sword in the troll's head.

The beast clawed at the scimitar. Its scaly grip locked around the weapon's cross hilt and tried to pull it free of the bone, but its strength was failing fast. Krusk stepped directly in front of the beast and raised his axe. The troll's horrid screech drowned the whistle of the axe until the blade sliced through the neck, just below Vadania's sword. The headless body tumbled sideways as the head, its eyes still rolling and the jaws snapping, rolled to Krusks's feet.

"The fire!" Vadania yelled.

Krusk picked up the head and held it at arm's length. The mass of skin writhed around his fingers as he carried it across the clearing and tossed it into the blaze. The stink of burning flesh fouled the area as flames licked up the troll's face. The flesh blackened, smoked, and split before the troll's eyes finally stopped rolling from side to side and only a blackened skull remained.

The others quickly hacked the body to pieces as it thrashed on the ground, knowing that within minutes it could regenerate even its lost skull and brain. The oozing parts were dragged or kicked into the firepit. Within minutes, all traces of the beast were gone, except for bloodstains on the ground and an unbearable stench in the air.

"What manner of beast was that?" Krusk asked as he shoved his axe into the fire.

Orange flames engulfed the blade, spitting and hissing as the thick, green blood coating its surface was consumed. Lidda moved about the camp, looking for bits of the creature.

"Troll," she said. "The bad news, there's likely to be more."

Vadania knelt by Malthooz's side. The half-orc was wedged into a tangle of roots where he lay all through the fight. His pupils were huge and his skin was even more ashen than its normal, gray hue. She waved her hand in front of his face. Malthooz stared past the druid, as though he was looking at something in the distance, or nothing at all.

"He's in shock," Vadania announced, placing her palm on his forehead.

She muttered softly over the half-orc's body and he relaxed, the calm spreading downward from his face as the druid's healing magic took effect.

"That should calm his nerves," she said, and she joined her companions near the fire. Looking at the charred ends of bones lying amidst the embers, she added, "I've no mind to pass the night here, but he needs to rest before we press on. He's had quite a scare."

Krusk pushed past Vadania and grabbed Malthooz, lifting him from the ground.

"I'll carry him," Krusk said. "We can't face another of those things."

He wrapped his arm under Malthooz's and heaved the limp form over his shoulder, then moved off. Vadania started after the barbarian but Mialee's hand pulled her back.

"He's right," she said.

Lidda passed by the druid, her backpack over her shoulder, her short sword and crossbow slung over her back. Vadania watched the rogue follow Krusk into the darkness. She lifted Mialee's hand from her own and grabbed her things.

"We've got to do something about that one," the druid said.

"Krusk or Malthooz?" Mialee asked as she started down the trail.

Vadania thought for a moment before answering, "Both."

They moved as fast as the situation allowed. Krusk was not slowed much by the extra weight, and Vadania knew that he was still working off the steam of battle. For all his outward gruffness, the druid did notice that the barbarian shielded Malthooz from the branches that hung across the trail and moved him carefully around the fallen trees that lay across the path.

She felt a growing affinity for Malthooz even though he was proving to be more trouble than he was worth. She also understood the frustration that he felt with Krusk. It was a frustration all of them dealt with from time to time. They'd learned to take the barbarian's temperament in stride. Vadania couldn't imagine the brute without his crotchety attitude. It was his essential characteristic, even if it was an exhausting trait. Still, for all of his grouchiness, Krusk was a rock of reliability in a world of shifting alliances. His dependability was unwavering and his bark far worse than his bite, provided you were on the right side of his axe.

Malthooz was a different matter. Something about his stubbornness reminded the druid of Krusk. There was no reason why he should be with them, and he was learning that the world of hired swords was more dangerous than he ever imagined. Yet he had chosen to come along, still believing that he could get Krusk to go home with him. The druid admired the principle behind Malthooz's determination. He was putting his own neck on the line for the sake of his people.

Vadania thought that she understood the kinship between the half-orcs. She would never call it love, at least on Krusk's part, but it was certainly real. The barbarian showed no genuine need for close emotional ties. His quick temper, however, sometimes betrayed something deeper. The only people who ever felt it were bitter enemies and close friends. Malthooz had to fall into the latter category.

As the night pressed on, Vadania sensed that the forest was changing around them. She caught the scent of salt in the air and knew that the ocean was not far off. She was tired beyond belief and needed rest if she hoped to use her magic in the days ahead. Waves of fatigue moved through her muscles and her mind was clouded with the strain of their flight.

She moved ahead to confer with the others, and they decided to pass the remaining hours of darkness on the edge of the coast away from the forest and another attack from its numerous dangers.

The druid used the promise of rest to keep her moving the final few miles. Even Krusk looked as if he needed sleep, she thought, as they cleared the edge of the forest and collapsed on the sand.

6

The morning sun burned through the fog shrouding
the beaches of the northern Fell Coast, bringing with it the
promise of a warmer day. White sand formed a gentle slope
stretching away on their left, meeting the ocean a hundred
yards beyond.

Vadania thought they should have journeyed farther into
the woods, but Mialee and Lidda were eager to leave the darkness behind and Krusk didn't want to waste time looking for
another path. The druid's eyes strayed skyward every few
minutes.

"We would be wise to stay near the forest edge," she said,
her voice flat.

"Rocs," she added, in answer to Malthooz's puzzled look.
"Giant and vicious avians that frequent coastal areas. They
scavenge by day and eat anything. The sea cliffs to the north
are probably filled with them."

The half-orc shuddered, looking at the towering walls of
stone in the distance. The encounter with the troll was still
fresh in his mind.

"If we keep to the cover of the trees we will be all right," Vadania said. "Most of the birds have migrated south by this time of year. Only the few too old to leave remain." She glanced up again. "They are still deadly, however."

They camped on the beach that evening. Vadania didn't think they were in any danger after dark. Even so, they camped under a low-hanging tree in the crook of two large logs of driftwood.

Malthooz sat away from the fire and the others, his back turned to them. He could hear Mialee and Lidda talking to Krusk in hushed tones. From the sound of it, it was not a pleasant conversation. Malthooz guessed that they were scolding the barbarian about his attitude, which had not improved since the fight in the woods. Whatever the case, he didn't think that any of them would pay much heed to him.

He grabbed the worn leather backpack that sat in front of him and drew it up between his booted feet, then rummaged through books and parchments to get at the wooden symbol lying in the bottom of the pack. The words of the disciple of Pelor who gave it to him ran through his head: "You lack faith, Malthooz. Faith in what you are."

His hands fell upon the uneven surface of the small wooden disc. He pulled it from the pack and set it on the ground at his feet. The center was raised in the pattern of a rising sun. It was a simple design but it was crafted to flow with the natural grain of the tree it was made from. Its simplicity was beautiful. The cleric told him that the symbol was a key to his power. As much as Malthooz wanted to believe it, he still just saw it as a lifeless chunk of wood.

The sound of footsteps in the sand behind him alerted Malthooz. He threw the symbol into his pack and tossed the bag aside.

"Still rummaging through those books?" Lidda's voice broke the stillness. She came up behind Malthooz and placed a hand upon his shoulder. "Come on, none of us likes this gloom and doom." She chuckled and ran a hand through the half-orc's unkempt hair. "Krusk is getting to be unbearable even to Mialee."

Malthooz sighed and said, "I failed myself and I failed you, Lidda. My stupidity almost cost me my life. I cannot forgive myself for such idiocy."

"Idiocy is what we're all about. Risking our necks for a few gold coins here and there."

Vadania left her seat by the fire and approached them.

"Lighten up on yourself, Malthooz, you'll get used to failing. I did."

"Yeah," Lidda added. "Anyway, Vadania and I have decided that you need some lessons—a few tricks and techniques with that stick of yours."

Malthooz laughed. He looked at the two women, their toned muscles rippling in the firelight. His eyes strayed to the scimitar strapped to Vadania's side.

"No, we won't start there," she said, unhooking the weapon from her belt and setting it on a nearby root. "We'll start small."

She hunted around for a long and slender piece of driftwood.

"Grab your staff," she said, testing the weight of her own pole. "Now put it up like this."

Malthooz tried to mimic the druid's stance, feet wide with his staff held crosswise across his chest.

"Now," Vadania said, coming at him, "step into my advance and raise your staff to block mine. Good."

They ran him through a battery of simple maneuvers, showing him the basic techniques of quarterstaff fighting. While the women each favored a different tool for battle, they were both handy enough with the pole to give Malthooz a few rudimentary skills. The three of them parried back and forth across the sand, exchanging mock blows with their wooden staves. It was not long before Malthooz was out of breath and had a number of dark bruises, more colorful than painful, on his sides. The elves had not broken a sweat.

"Enough," Malthooz hollered, falling to the sand. "Enough!"

"Bah," Krusk's deep voice boomed from the fireside. He had watched the sparring lessons with quiet disdain. "You wouldn't last a second in a real battle if you tire that quickly."

He grabbed Malthooz's staff from the sand and started forward.

"Get up," Krusk shouted as he bore down on Malthooz.

Malthooz scrambled to his feet but was too slow to avoid Krusk's lightning-quick swing. The staff cracked across his shoulder, snapping at the point where it hit his shoulder blade. The half-orc stepped back in shock but managed to keep his footing. Though pain bolted through his arm, he refused to let it show on his face.

The half-orcs stood face-to-face for many moments, their eyes burning with the rage of a rekindled rivalry. Malthooz sneered.

"It is no different than it ever has been, is it, Krusk?" he asked.

Krusk tossed the splintered ends of the staff to the ground and stormed off.

When Malthooz awoke the next morning, the ache in his shoulder reminded him of the furious confrontation the night before. He knew that Krusk hadn't meant to fly off in such frenzy and guessed that Krusk's anger was probably directed more against his own conflicted feelings about returning to the village than against anything Malthooz had done. He was also certain that Krusk's actions, however antagonistic they might seem, were really a sign that he did care about what was happening to his friends of long ago.

Malthooz rubbed his sore muscles. If this was Krusk's way of showing love, so be it. It was better than the silent treatment

Malthooz had endured during the journey up till then. The standoff seemed to bring the two to a mutual understanding. Malthooz was pleased with himself for not backing down. Perhaps it was only stupid pride. It was painful pride for sure. It was also a start.

More than anything else, it showed Malthooz that the only way he could make Krusk consider the request was to relate to him on Krusk's terms. There was nothing new about that, but it was easy to forget such lessons over the years.

Malthooz rose from his bedroll and started packing his things. Lidda and Krusk were hiding the remains of the camp. They kicked sand over the smoldering embers of the night's fire and smoothed the sand with pine branches.

Vadania was nowhere to be seen. Malthooz guessed that she was off in the forest, gathering food for the day's journey or herbs for healing or casting spells. Once they left the woodlands for the open beach and cliffs, such things would be much harder to come by.

Mialee sat against the trunk of a tree, poring over her spellbook, memorizing the spidery script that flowed across the pages in a way that allowed wizards to access the magical secrets held within the words, diagrams, and formulae.

Malthooz looked around for the broken ends of his walking staff. The fractured pieces of wood were nowhere to be seen. He finished rolling his bedding and tying it shut with a length of silk cord. As he carried the bundle over to his backpack and began strapping it to the underside of the bag, something caught his eye. A long, lean staff of wood rested against his pack. Lying next to the staff was a shorter and much sturdier-looking piece. The surface of the smaller weapon was worked smooth and it tapered down its length from one end to the other.

Malthooz finished tying his bedroll in place and hefted his backpack to his shoulder, wincing as the weight of it pressed on the bruise beneath. He paused for a moment then took off his pack and rummaged around for the symbol of Pelor. He hung the trinket from a leather cord around his neck, tucking it inside his tunic. After re-donning his pack, Malthooz slid the club into his belt and grabbed the new staff. The weapons felt balanced and reassuring.

For the first time in a long time, Malthooz greeted the coming day with confidence.

They traveled north along the sand well into the morning. The forest to the east slowly gave way to sandy bluff then to a jagged wall of stone. The beach disappeared as the tide came in, forcing the group to climb a number of low rises where huge sea stacks trailed out into the surf. By the time the sun reached its crest in the sky, the water finally started receding and travel became easier.

Rippling water lapped at the heels of Krusk's boots as the companions rounded a final peak of rock and got their first view of the broken ship.

Despite the lateness of the day, a thin fog had settled over the beach, the winter sun unable to shake its hold on the shore. The mist obscured sight at any distance greater than a quarter mile and gave the whole scene a ghostly aspect.

As they moved closer, Krusk could begin making out the details of the wreckage. *Treachery* lay on the beach as though she had been tossed as a giant's plaything. A gash split one side of the hull where it was impaled on the rocks. The mast was a tangle of splintered timber and snarled lines, and the rudder was nowhere to be seen. A few large crates were strewn around the craft, those too heavy for the sea to have claimed as its own. Already the boat was sinking into the sand. The smell of salty air mixed with something else more putrid.

"I don't like this," Krusk said, eyeing the wreck. "It smells of death, but I see no bodies."

"I think we're a bit late for whatever happened here," Lidda said. "I'd guess that Vadania's rocs beat us to the dead."

"Or they've been washed away," the druid added.

"We should split up," Mialee declared, stepping forward to join the other two. "The tide's going to turn before long. We can cover more ground in teams."

Krusk nodded and said, "I don't think there's any danger in that. Whatever happened to the crew is long done."

"Good," Mialee said. "I'll take the half-orcs and check the inside." She adjusted a pouch of herbs on her belt. "Lidda should go topside and Vadania can search the beach for tracks."

The railing at the rear of the ship hung half a dozen yards above the surface of the sand. A grappling hook and rope made the ascent as easy for Lidda as a climb up a short flight of stairs, and she reached the edge of the deck in seconds. Grabbing the top with both hands, she vaulted up and over it, landing in a crouch on well-worn planks. She snatched the crossbow from its holster on her back and advanced down the ship's length.

She moved stealthily along the deck, gliding around the perimeter of the vessel, riffling past folds of cloth from the fallen sail. She rummaged through a few boxes that were lashed to the deck at various points as she made her way to the bow.

Most of the containers were smashed open, with yards of heavy canvas, hemp rope, and an assortment of pulleys spilling from their insides.

From the open deck, it looked as though a hurricane had hit the ship. What remained of the mainmast was no more than a short, jagged stump protruding from the decking. Rivets still held the stub firmly to a steel collar where the post emerged from belowdecks. The lower end of the once towering pole presumably still ran down through the heart of the craft and butted the keel. The rest of its length lay across the deck, flattening a section of railing near the front of the boat, with its final yards hanging over the beach.

A boulder was partially sunk into the deck near the base of the fractured mainmast. What showed of the stone was perfectly round. Nothing short of a catapult could have hurled such a thing.

Whatever had happened, Lidda thought, I'm alone on deck now and there's no sign of the crew anywhere.

She returned the crossbow to its holster on her back and made her way back through the jumble of rigging toward her grappling line.

The fissure in the hull was large enough for the half-orcs to walk through upright. Krusk went through first, followed by Malthooz then Mialee. The space they entered was dimly lit by sunlight coming through the gap in the hull, but it was enough to see the remains of battered crates and barrels littering the sloping floor.

"Looks to me like the place has been ransacked," Krusk said, tossing aside a broken plank.

"From the stains on the insides of these barrels," Mialee said, sniffing a crimson-stained stave from a crushed barrel,

"I'd say this was some expensive wine. Whoever or whatever was here first, obviously had no class."

"Nor taste for fine food," Malthooz added, examining round wheels of cheese and dried chunks of meat.

"Maybe not," Krusk said as he tossed a chunk of meat to Malthooz.

The dried flank was riddled with tiny bite marks.

Mialee grabbed a dagger from her belt and said, "Probably just rats, but let's be careful."

"Bah," Krusk said.

As if in response to his grunt, a crossbow bolt hit the wooden beam near his head with a thud. A second flew past Malthooz, grazing his arm before slamming into the side of the hull.

Mialee crouched and drew her short bow from her shoulder.

"There," she yelled, pointing to the doorway on the far side of the room.

A small, dog-faced head pulled back from the doorframe. Krusk leaped over the crate in front of him and chased after the creature, following the sound of its bare feet slapping against the planking. Mialee was right on his heels.

Krusk swung his axe around the corner before the rest of his body was even through the door. He felt the blade pass through the soft flesh of the creature's body before thudding into the wall. The barbarian moved into the hallway, yanking his weapon free as he did.

The stench from the creature's body wrinkled Krusk's nose with disgust. The scent was unmistakable — kobold. He spat, hoping to rid his mouth of the odor. A pack of the tiny things might be a challenge, he thought as he watched two more of the beasts round a corner farther down the passage. Only a handful of the wretches, however, would be a shame to kill. Krusk glanced at the scaly body lying at his feet and reminded himself of the races' penchant for cruelty, their tendency to pick on those weaker than themselves, and their frequent raids on human villages. He bolted after the kobolds, amending his last thought as he went. Not killing them would be a shame.

By the time the kobolds realized their mistake it was too late. A pile of overturned crates blocked the corridor they'd run down. The rope that previously held the crates to the walls dangled loosely from iron rings in the wall. As Krusk came around the corner, the kobolds growled and barked, backing themselves into the heap of broken wood. Krusk swatted away the miniature spear that was thrust at him and brought his axe down, leveling both kobolds with a single blow.

"Damn, Krusk," Mialee said as she came around the corner, "couldn't you have saved one for me?"

Malthooz was just behind the wizard.

"They smell awful," he said, his words muffled by the hand he held over his nose. "I've heard stories, but have never seen one up close. They look harmless enough."

He rolled one of the child-sized bodies over with his boot. The creature looked something like a cross between a lizard and a dog. He knelt beside the body for a closer look.

"Don't let their size fool you," Mialee said, "a pack of them can level a small community in minutes. A whole tribe, a few hundred of them, can take a town. Let's be careful, there's probably more."

"It'll take more than that to slow us down," Krusk said as he wiped his axe blade on a plank of wood. "Let's find that magic stick. There's another passage on the other side of that storeroom."

As he started back toward the cargo hold, Krusk felt the flooring jolt as though something had struck the ship.

"The tide couldn't have come in that fast," Mialee said as she moved to join the barbarian at the junction of hallways.

The side of the craft exploded behind Malthooz. Fragments of hull sailed past Krusk as he fought to keep his footing.

Malthooz, caught by the full force of the blast, was flung into the far wall. His head slammed against a low beam and he fell to the floor. A hail of broken wood showered his unmoving form as a massive claw burst through the hull.

Lidda was nearly to her hook and line when she heard the crash and felt the impact. The deck trembled as reverberations from the blow traveled through the sun-bleached wood.

Her grappling hook forgotten, Lidda leaped over the side of the ship in one fluid motion and prepared herself for a soft landing on the beach. By the time her feet made contact, the crossbow was held tightly in her grip. Her finger twitched on the trigger as she moved around the side of *Treachery*.

As she rounded the starboard edge of the ship, she heard an unmistakable sound. It was the deep howl that would make anyone who knew him painfully aware that Krusk was mad.

8

Malthooz felt himself slipping away from conscious-
ness. He was aware of pain from something hitting his
shoulder and he felt his neck whip as his upper body impacted
the wall. His head collided sharply with a large beam. The
pain was intense at first, taking the breath from his lungs,
but it quickly dulled as he faded toward unconsciousness.
The pain in his skull subsided to an ache. The world stopped
spinning around him and he felt himself being laid gently
to rest.

When he awoke, Malthooz found himself inside an immense
and intensely white chamber. The marble floor and walls
where polished to a high shine, matching the luminescent,
alabaster columns that ran in rows the length of the room. The
pillars held aloft a vaulted, half-globe ceiling.

The interior curve of the ceiling was inlayed with multi-
colored stones, shorn flat and laid into an amazing mosaic
of images. At the four cardinal directions were shield-sized
orange spheres with tendrils of yellow and red radiating from
them. These suns were laid into an obsidian background and

almost glowed in contrast to the midnight hues of the burnished, ebony stone.

Set in the center of the picture was the image of an enormous dragon. The outline of the dragon's scales was done with emeralds and lapis, and the whole of the thing was covered in gold leaf. In its talons, the creature clutched a silver mace topped with yet another orange-red sun.

Spaced evenly around the image of the dragon were several smaller figures, knights in full plate armor holding aloft long swords in homage to the beast. On each of the knights' breastplates was an inlay of the same solar motif repeated elsewhere.

Malthooz was lying flat on his back on the floor of the temple, staring up at the image above him. He shook his head. He remembered something striking him. He reached up and rubbed his skull. There were no lumps or bruises as far as he could tell.

He sat up, pushing himself into a sitting position with his elbows. The makeshift club lay at his side along with the symbol of Pelor. He didn't remember taking the talisman into the ship with him. What became of the ship, and why had he been there in the first place? That seemed so long ago. He remembered traveling with Krusk and some others. Perhaps the journey had been nothing but a dream. On the other hand, he didn't recognize this place at all, so maybe this was the dream.

Despite his confusion over where he was and how he got there, Malthooz felt clear-headed and alert. He considered for a moment that he might be dead, but discarded the notion. This place did not look like the paradise of wilderness and plenty the shamans promised.

Without thinking, he grabbed the wooden symbol. His whole body convulsed as his fingers wrapped around the trinket. A surge of energy ran from the symbol through his hand and along his arm. His head snapped back as the wave traveled up his spine. Malthooz shut his eyes against a flood of tears, but they could not be halted.

A moment later the energy stopped, and the symbol of Pelor clattered to the ground. A flood of emotions and memories hit Malthooz all at once. Feelings long pent up suddenly rushed forth: wounds of humiliation at the hands of his childhood peers; having to watching his village suffer failed crops and the raids of bandits; the pain he'd felt when Krusk moved on, and his anger at himself for not being brave enough to leave himself. All of those feelings came and passed.

Malthooz stared at the wooden symbol. The words of the acolyte of Pelor echoed in his mind. "You lack faith in yourself." Then more of the things he had been told came back. Some were things he had tried to forget: that a deity's call was not one of choice and that it was useless to resist. Malthooz had resisted from the start, and continued to fight it. He ran from his village, having convinced himself that he wanted only to find Krusk, thinking that if he could convince Krusk to return, everything would be all right and his heart would be at peace. He was beginning to understand how wrong he was.

Mialee reacted reflexively. Her hand shot toward the claw as the familiar words of a spell came to her lips. Three bolts of light and energy flew from her outstretched fingers and raced at the appendage, slamming into its armored side. The yellow glow of the missiles dissipated against the claw, sending arcs of electricity racing along its rough surface, but doing it no visible damage.

She cursed under her breath as the tendrils of magic faded into the surface of the armor. Realizing that she had only a few seconds before the rest of the creature came bursting into the hold, she grabbed Malthooz by the collar and pulled his body down the hall with all her strength. Mialee was thankful that the passage of many years and feet had worn the floor to a smooth polish. Nevertheless, strength was not one of the elf's primary virtues, and the strain of dragging the half-orc's bulk taxed her muscles to the limit of her endurance.

Krusk was already moving forward by the time Mialee loosed her ineffective magic. He was upon the beast before she pulled Malthooz safely from the claw's reach. Heat burned in his chest and a hum filled his ears. The rage of battle infused him and he welcomed the feeling, hungering for the rush that a good fight brought. His axe felt like an extension of his arm as he moved in on the monster.

A second claw reached into the hallway, grabbing the jagged edge of the hole and wrenching away more timber. A pair of legs came through the hole, followed by another. Soon the entire bulk of a giant crab filled the narrow passageway. Its mouth was a dark complex of tiny mandibles and jaw plates that popped and clicked as they opened and closed. It must have been lurking in the shallow water, Krusk thought as he swung his axe at a leg that speared toward his throat. Krusk could guess why there were no bodies in the wreck.

"You'll not take this meal so easily as the corpse of a dead, bloated sailor," Krusk howled as he brought his axe back around on the crab.

He was deep in the throes of his rage and cared little for the fact that the monster couldn't understand him. His weapon smashed into one of the crab's armored claws with a crunch, shattering the plating near the tip, sending small bits of shell flying back into the barbarian's face.

The monster moved toward Krusk, responding to the

immediate threat. It lashed out at the barbarian with both claws, the wound from Krusk's axe barely slowing it. Krusk knew little of sea creatures but he suspected that the beast could not feel pain.

The crab snapped at Krusk as he tried to land a second strike. The inner surface of its claws looked like a rough landscape of calcified matter. They didn't look sharp but the barbarian knew that what they lacked in edge, they made up for in sheer strength. He was more than aware that either of them could easily sever his arm once it locked on. To be caught by both was unthinkable. Krusk bided his time, looking for the opportunity to hit, knowing that the monster would neither rest nor be frightened away.

Mialee dropped Malthooz a few yards from the crab's back. She tossed her short bow aside, realizing the futility of using the weapon against the creature's tough exoskeleton. She thought her staff would be equally useless, except perhaps as a distraction to the crab so she abandoned it as well and prepared to cast another spell.

Against such a mindless beast, magical charms and enchantments would be of no use. Her magic missiles already demonstrated their futility. She realized that Krusk was their best hope of surviving the attack and she set about to bolster the half-orc's offensive power. If the barbarian was going to stand a chance against the monster's multiple weapons, he was going to need more than just his axe and a little luck.

She concentrated on Krusk's movements, watching his every move and getting herself in tune with his every step and shift. Grabbing a piece of licorice root from a pouch at her side, she shifted part of her awareness to the twig. Her mouth worked the words of the spell, her delivery becoming louder and more sure as the magic took effect. Speaking the final word, Mialee shifted her attention back to Krusk and sent forth a conjuration of energy.

Krusk felt the potency of the magic coursing through his veins. Even in his enraged state, the warmth of the magic infused his movements and brought an extra quickness to his attacks. He redoubled his efforts. One of the creature's legs let go with a snap as Krusk's axe severed it near the joint. The remaining stub twitched and jerked, rendered all but useless with the loss of its pointed tip. Krusk concentrated his attacks on the smaller appendages between warding off the lunging claws.

Beast and barbarian danced back and forth down the tiny hallway. The sound of Krusk's booted footsteps was lost amidst the clacking of the monster's legs on the wooden floor. Krusk was lost in a passionate rage of survival, his actions marked by instinct that rivaled that of the crab. Time and again he landed blows on the creature. The salty smell of sea water oozed from cracks and fissures in the crab's outer skeleton. Bits of soft, pink meat hung from the holes. Still the beast came like a relentless automaton.

Mialee struck at the creature's hind legs. She had little hope of causing any real injury, but her rapid assault forced the crab to skitter to keep its balance.

Finally, Krusk took off one of the claws with a mighty swing. That created an opening in the monster's defense and allowed Krusk to shift his attacks toward the crab's belly and the softer shell beneath its mouth, where another strike deep into the underside of the creature gave Krusk his victory.

The monster convulsed and crashed to the floor, its remaining legs crumpled and knotted beneath its bulk.

Krusk and Mialee both rushed to Malthooz's side. Mialee grabbed his wrist and felt the weak beat of his heart through the artery there.

"He's alive," she said, dropping Malthooz's limp arm, "and pretty damn lucky, I'd say."

"His luck will run out at some point," Krusk spat, "and I don't want his death on my head."

"Any one of us would have been caught off guard and felled by that blow. If you're going to be so damn glib about his lack of skill, why don't you check that ego of yours and teach him to fight?"

"He'll never learn."

"He won't if you don't give him the chance, you oaf!" someone else said.

They both turned and saw Lidda standing at the intersection of the hallway.

Krusk looked away, avoiding the rogue's gaze. He knew that what the women said was true. He really did yearn to tell Malthooz more about himself and his life, but his own stubbornness always seemed to get in the way. He grabbed his unconscious companion under the arms and lifted him from the floor.

"I tried to help," Lidda explained, "but by the time I made my way around the ship, the excitement was done and there was no way I was getting in behind that thing. I don't know that I could have done much against that armor anyway."

Krusk felt the heat of the battle flowing from his body, replaced by weariness. He was spent and would have to rest again before he did anything strenuous.

"Come on," he said, "let's get out of here before something else tries to eat us."

9

A hawk soared high above the bluff that rose from the eastern edge of the coast, wheeling on a warm blast of heated air
radiating from the rocks below, using the thermal current to
gain altitude. Wind rustled through the feathers of the creature's broad wings, whispering slightly as it made its way over
the tiny hairs at their tips.

The bird circled, taking in the general lay of the land. Its
eyes pierced a shroud of fog, darting over the expanse of beach
below. Figures moved across the sand. The creatures posed no
threat to the hawk as far as she could tell. Nothing in the
area did. Even the huge birds of prey that sometimes hunted
there would leave her alone. She was too small to be of much
interest to them.

As she wheeled higher into the air, the hawk watched
a few of the humans pass into a dark mass they had been
scurrying around, and another of them scaled its side.
There was something about them that registered in her
mind, triggering vague memories and a feeling of kinship
and familiarity.

Vadania welcomed any excuse to take to wing. She lost herself in the thrill of flight and reveled in the pull of instinct, giving up a part of her rational mind for a more ancient kind of knowing. She did not entirely lose touch with who or what she was, but everything came to her through a different lens of understanding. She passed over the ship once and pulled up into a steep climb.

While she was probably the most suited of the party to pick up on any trails that were left behind, Vadania knew tracking was not her greatest skill. She could use her shapechanging abilities, heightened senses of sight or smell, or in this case flight, to great advantage. They did the druid little good, however, if she didn't know what to look for aside from the most obvious indication of someone's passing.

The beach yielded little information. Vadania expected this, given the play of the tides and the shifting nature of its fine sands. Waves would erase any evidence of passage within hours of their being left. The trail grew more promising, however, when she ascended the bluff.

Near its top, she spotted unmistakable signs that a group had recently been camped there. Evidence of multiple fire pits and charred chunks of deer or elk were strewn across the ground. Vadania felt her anger rising at the lack of respect shown the animals' remains, even if they were just a meal. An equal lack of concern marked the trail of prints that ran from the site and into the scrub forest to the east. A blind gnome could have followed the trail. A sickly stench lingered on the breeze. She followed the trail for a little while, then turned back when it was apparent that whatever left it was at least a few days gone.

As she flew back out over the beach, Vadania saw that her companions were returning from the ship. She watched them setting a camp near the foot of the bluff, looking like insects from her height. Smoke drifted lazily from a small fire ring while she watched their tiny forms move about the scene. As the druid descended, she could make out each of her friends in clearer and clearer detail.

Krusk hunkered over the fire, tossing pieces of driftwood onto the sputtering flames. Lidda dug through her pack, probably looking for food. Mialee sat on the beach next to Malthooz's prone form, her hand upon the half-orc's brow. He looked dead. Were it not for the attention Mialee paid him, Vadania would have concluded he was.

Her descent grew more rapid. She approached the party in a steep dive, flaring her tail feathers at the last second to slow her approach. She landed on the sand with a double hop. No one seemed very surprised by her appearance. The only one of them who hadn't witnessed her shapechanging was out cold. She let out a shrill shriek.

A transformation started in the depths of her chest. Her heart pulsed more slowly and the talons at the tips of her clawed feet began to expand and flatten. Her body grew rapidly to its full height as the feathers composing the hawk's wings withdrew into the pores on her arms. The beak pulled back into her face and her eyes grew into the long, almond shape that marked those of her race.

Within moments, an elf woman stood where the bird had been. Vadania reached down to reassure herself by touching the hilt of her scimitar. The weapon was strapped to her hip, as it should be. The antlers in her hair and the beads that covered her clothing were all as they had been an hour before.

"Is he all right?" she asked, joining Mialee at Malthooz's side.

The wooden symbol lay exposed on the half-orc's chest. She stared at the disk.

"Krusk found it on him when he drug him up here," Mialee said. "It's a holy symbol, eh?"

Vadania grabbed the disk, turning it over and nodding.

"Looks like a symbol to Pelor," said the druid. "I thought I saw him with it earlier."

"He took a blow to the head, but he'll be all right," Mialee said. "He's stirred a few times and groaned once or twice."

Vadania placed a hand on Malthooz's forehead, reciting the words to a simple healing spell.

"Someone was definitely here within the week," she said when the spell was done. "A large group I'd say, maybe a dozen and a half. I don't think they were from the ship. I don't think they were even human, in fact, though I'm not sure."

Krusk grunted and cracked open a chunk of crab leg that he was roasting over the fire. He tossed a piece of it to the women.

"Tried to eat us," he explained, "so it only seemed fair to return the favor."

"In the ship?" Vadania asked.

"Between this and a couple of kobolds," the barbarian said between mouthfuls, "we were busy."

"The kobolds must have been in there a while. I didn't find any tracks," Vadania said. "Either way, I doubt the staff is still here."

Lidda joined them near the fire and said, "Krusk and I went back in for a thorough search after we got Malthooz out."

"Nothing," Krusk said with disgust.

"There's more, though," Lidda said. "That boat wasn't run aground by a storm. It was attacked. Someone put a boulder the size of a bugbear through the mast. The way I see it, if we follow the trail you found up into the hills, we'll find what we're after." A grin crept across her face. "I'd wager that old wizard is good for a few more coins if we go through the extra trouble."

"If the guild doesn't take too big a cut," Krusk said. "I like this job less and less."

Malthooz groaned and stirred. Soon he sat up, rubbing his head.

"Where . . . ?"

Krusk handed him a piece of crabmeat. "We were attacked and you were knocked out," he said.

There was a definite edge to his words, but Vadania ignored the barbarian's tone.

"How do you feel?" she asked.

"My head is splitting," Malthooz replied. He moved his arms in wide circles, flexing his hands open and closed. "I think I'm all right, though."

Vadania pointed at the symbol around his neck and asked, "Where did you get that?"

Malthooz stuffed the symbol back under his shirt.

"I think," he began, then shook his head. "It's not clear . . . more like a dream."

A thick fog settled in as the sun fell. They ate more of the crab, savoring the fresh meat. It was a welcome change from their diet of dried rations, and would help them to conserve their dwindling supplies. That was something they had to consider, with a longer journey ahead than they'd anticipated.

Malthooz awoke as a ray of sunlight burned through the fog and landed on his closed eyes. The brightness shining through his eyelids chased the sleep from his mind. Vadania tended a small fire. She'd taken the last watch. An earthy smell wafted from a kettle suspended over the blaze, hanging from a makeshift tripod of driftwood. She watched Malthooz rise and poured him a mug of brown tea.

"It's not much to chew on," she said, handing it to him, "but it will chase the chill from your bones."

He took a drink. It was bitter, but not unpleasant.

"I remember now what happened yesterday," he said.

The druid set her mug down.

"You were visited," she said. It was not a question. She spoke as though she already knew what had happened to him. "I noticed the symbol back at the inn. I wasn't sure you knew what it was at the time. I am now."

He told her about the time he'd spent with the cleric and about the things he'd been taught, how he'd been told that he was chosen by Pelor and that it wasn't really up to him one way or another. Vadania listened to his story, nodding occasionally but otherwise keeping quiet. When he was finished, they sat in silence for a few minutes.

Vadania finally spoke. "Your only choice now is whether you heed the calling or not." She smiled. "It could be worse."

"Could it?" Malthooz asked, looking into the empty mug in his hands.

The others soon rose. Camp was broken after a quick meal of leftover crabmeat. Malthooz was surprised by how much Krusk's demeanor had changed since the previous evening.

"He almost appears to be looking forward to the journey," Lidda remarked as she slung her crossbow across her shoulder.

"Yeah, but don't ask him about his change of heart. You might upset him again," Malthooz replied jokingly, though he kept his voice down.

"I don't know," the rogue responded, watching Krusk kick sand over the glowing embers from the fire. "I think he and the druid had some words last night." She grinned. "Whatever she said, she finally got something through to the oaf. Nonetheless, we probably shouldn't push it."

The climb up to the top of the bluff took hours, but wasn't overly difficult. The scene at the top was as the druid described. Blackened deer carcasses and piles of frayed bones littered the area. It didn't look so much like a camp as the place where a pack of wild dogs had sheltered. Tattered bits of clothing were mixed in with the other trash.

"Poor bastard," Krusk said, tossing aside the torn sleeve of a sailor's jacket. Embroidery of gold and silver thread made a pattern of bars on the shoulder. "I doubt that death came swiftly for this unfortunate soul."

"I don't think we're doing ourselves any favors hanging around here," Lidda said. "We should move on. I'd like to be as far from here as possible by nightfall."

"Yes, the neglect and disrespect pains my soul even more seeing it up close," Vadania said.

Krusk set his boot down inside a large set of footprints. The depression dwarfed the half-orc's foot by inches. Numerous sets of smaller prints ran alongside them. All pointed east, back into the forest.

"Not many people venture into the Deepwood this far north," Vadania said, "even among the daring."

Her words sent a shiver through Malthooz.

The druid led them along the trail. Mialee followed close behind her. Malthooz and Krusk walked behind the wizard and Lidda covered the rear, her crossbow drawn.

"Don't you ever tire of keeping your guard like that, Lidda?" Mialee asked.

"I let my guard down once. I will never make that mistake again," the rogue replied.

She lifted her leather armor, exposing a jagged scar on her abdomen.

Malthooz was learning that the rogue was not half so serious as she seemed most of the time. She had a quick wit and was not afraid to use it. Still, it was a bit unnerving the way she could change so quickly, not unlike Krusk. One minute she was joking and the next she was poised to kill. He realized how valuable that was in a profession where a moment's hesitation meant death or imprisonment. Having spent only a matter of days with the woman, he considered her one of the few people to whom he would trust his life. But the same went for any of the others. Malthooz was beginning to understand how the life of adventure had drawn Krusk and how the bonds of camaraderie held them together. They might bicker during quiet times, but they would watch each others' backs when it counted.

A chill wind swept south across the region as the day wore on and they followed the trail across the barren land. It was an inhospitable place, bordered by high mountain ranges to the north. To the south, open plains were just visible beyond the reaches of Deepwood. If the tracks kept straight on, they would enter the forest a half-day's journey ahead.

Scrub yielded slowly to the woodlands. Stunted trees dotted the scenery and low, woody bushes became more frequent. It was not a pleasant place to be, and the isolation of the landscape was made even more oppressive by the evidence of their quarry's passage. Shrubs were trampled flat. Saplings had been uprooted. The ground was mired with muddy snow. It was little consolation that the muck made the trail easy to follow. Even the few yellow flowers they saw poking up between mounds of slush did little to dispel the severe feel of the place.

The pursuers stopped at midday to rest and eat. Krusk badgered Vadania to look for something tastier than trail rations, but she wouldn't do it, arguing that she would not further upset the balance of nature in the face of so much wanton destruction.

Malthooz took his club from his belt to practice the moves that the women had taught him. He saw Krusk grab his axe and move toward him. Malthooz dropped his arm to his side.

"I talked to the druid," Krusk said, raising his axe. "I know about the symbol and your vision."

Malthooz was stunned, unable to read the barbarian's emotions. Krusk nodded to his club and Malthooz raised it in front of himself, spreading his legs to match Krusk's stance.

"The elves know how to fight," the barbarian said, "but they don't know how *we* fight."

He swung his axe around on a small tree. The blade sliced cleanly through the three-inch trunk, toppling it to the ground.

Krusk ignored the glare Vadania shot him and continued, "You must use your strength to your advantage. Put the whole of it into every strike. Overwhelm your enemies quickly and make sure they don't live long enough to strike back." He rested the head of his axe on the ground and added, "I am not going back to the village."

"I know that," Malthooz said, nodding.

"Just so we're clear."

Krusk walked back to where the others were seated. Malthooz followed him over.

"It was really more an audience than a vision, I think. I saw this," Malthooz said, reaching into the neck of his tunic and drawing forth the wooden symbol. "I felt something coursing through me that I've never felt the likes of before. It comes back, though much reduced in strength, when I touch this."

"A cleric?" Mialee asked, moving closer and taking the symbol from his hands. "It's certainly not like most of the symbols I've seen. They are generally made of silver or better."

"That may be, but whether that's a requirement of the god or of a cleric's vanity is an open question," Vadania said. "It is not unlike a fetish to the nature gods. Still, I agree that it is unusual for Pelor to grant favor to a half-orc."

"Bah," Krusk sputtered. "I think you're letting that blow go to your head. Gods! What good have they done for your village? All of the praying and ceremony of the zealots never stopped the worgs from carrying off livestock or children. Stick to the club. The wolves understand what a bash on the snout means."

Malthooz took the symbol back from the wizard and dropped it down the front of his tunic.

"Say what you will, Krusk. I don't expect you to understand."

Lidda appeared in the dense trees ahead. She was moving in a crouch, a finger over her mouth, signaling the others to keep quiet. Her cloak blended perfectly with the tree trunks as she moved silently toward them. Malthooz reached for his club to steady his shaking hand. He watched the others react to the rogue's return, tightening their own grips on the weapons they held ready. Krusk drummed his fingers in sequence along the handle of his axe. The sound only added to Malthooz's anxiousness.

Sleep had been difficult for the half-orc the previous night as the companions camped on the open plain. He spent most of it tossing and turning as nightmares of the troll chasing him ran endlessly through his head. Every sound that echoed from the nearby forest startled him wide awake. When he wasn't peering anxiously into the darkness, he was shivering under his coarse, wool blanket.

The light of day found him still weary and sore. No one wanted to light a fire for fear of attracting unwanted attention, though the damp, frigid air left Malthooz wishing for one.

They followed the footprints deeper into the forest for most of the morning. By noon there was still no sign of their quarry beyond the tracks they left behind. Tall pines and firs, standing over the group like sentinels, blocked most of the light of midday and brought a dismal feeling over the journey. At least the cover kept them out of the icy wind, though Malthooz would have welcomed its sound over the eerie silence that hung over the place.

"Gnolls ahead. A pair of them," Lidda said in an urgent whisper, holding up two fingers to emphasize the point. "About a quarter mile. They look half drunk."

Krusk's tapping stopped suddenly.

"Dog faces," he said with a sneer, "should be easy."

He started moving.

"I'm not so sure," Vadania said, grabbing his arm. "We don't know how many there are, or how organized they are."

"She's right," Mialee said. "What about the big footprints? Let's not get carried away until we know what we're up against."

"I'd guess that the rest of the group is somewhere ahead," Lidda said. "They must have a camp. I don't think they'd post guards if they were going anywhere."

"That's a fair guess, but I don't want to stake my life on it," Vadania said. "I'd be much more comfortable if we did more snooping. I shouldn't have too much trouble getting by them."

They all turned as Krusk buried the head of his axe in a tree trunk.

"Make your plans," he growled, "but be quick with it."

Vadania scowled at the barbarian. "There's precious little living in these parts as it is," she said.

Malthooz missed Vadania's transformation the previous day and he watched with fascination as her body changed. He tried to keep his eyes on the woman as it happened, but the process was difficult to track. The details were easy enough, the fur emerging from her skin and her fingernails becoming claws. It was the gross metamorphosis of form that made the half-orc queasy. He was not sure that he could describe what he was seeing. Vadania's body collapsed on itself as her muscles shrank and contracted. Her skin folded over and condensed. Fur sprouted from the tips and insides of her pointed ears.

Within moments, the elf woman Malthooz knew was nowhere to be seen. A squirrel twittered on the ground where she had been. The animal leaped onto a nearby tree trunk, making a quick circuit. She appeared on a branch high above, chirping and chattering at her companions on the ground. With a swish of her bushy tail, the druid jumped to another branch and darted into the woods.

The half-orc was thankful for the delay that the druid's scouting mission brought, even though he realized it was only temporary. A fight seemed inevitable at this point, and Malthooz was not overly eager to see it happen. He suspected that Krusk felt differently, guessing from the way he paced around, muttering curses into the air. It had always been that way with Krusk for as long as Malthooz knew him. Krusk had never been one for subtlety. He was the one who rushed headlong into whatever lay ahead, whether he knew what it was or not. Most often he didn't. Malthooz was glad for the presence of the druid and the other women. He'd hesitate to say that they made Krusk into a more sensible or gentle creature, but they did have a certain balancing affect on his reckless urges.

Something about Krusk's attitude was strangely infectious, though. Malthooz had never developed much physical prowess, but Krusk was different. Ever since he'd arrived at the village of outcasts, seeking a safe place to lay low, he'd been the best at anything involving strength, and Malthooz admired the attention it brought him.

Maybe he'd spent too much time with the barbarian,

Malthooz thought, watching as a combined glare from Lidda and Mialee made Krusk set his axe down and take a seat. Malthooz could not deny that he felt a small but growing part of himself that hoped for a fight. He would have thought that the encounter with the troll would have been sufficient to frighten him off. The nightmares were certainly terrifying enough. Strangely, it was having the opposite effect, and he wasn't sure why. As scared as he was, he felt like he had to face the fear head on. The only way he was going to do that was through battle.

Malthooz shook his head. Did he have any idea what he was saying to himself? He looked up and saw the druid approaching. He reached for the disk under his shirt to calm his fear and get a grip on his fluctuating emotions.

Vadania came striding through the trees, already reverted into her elf form. The druid's every movement echoed the gentle sway of the wind through the pines. Her natural adornments, the beads and shells in her hair and on her clothing, only added to Malthooz's sense that the woman was of the forest. She looked at home.

"The group is not far from here," Vadania reported, her voice low and her tone grim. "There's a clearing about a mile ahead. It contains many tents and a crude wooden building. Might be an abandoned bandit camp. Gnolls were crawling all over the place. I saw at least a dozen, and that's not including the guards Lidda saw. There's probably more in the woods." She dropped her eyes. "I don't think a frontal assault is the best choice."

Krusk was on his feet again. He grabbed his axe from a knot of roots and slammed it into the loop on his belt.

"Figures," he growled.

Lidda gave the barbarian a sympathetic look and said, "Sorry, Krusk."

Malthooz didn't know how much more idleness Krusk could take.

Lidda turned to the wizard and asked, "Mialee, can you work something on the guards?"

The wizard nodded and replied, "Why, do you have a plan?"

Malthooz saw Lidda's grin and knew that the rogue had something in mind. She gave the half-orc a wink.

"We should move back until after nightfall," she said. "My plan requires the right conditions."

Malthooz followed Krusk as the company retreated.

They moved out as darkness settled. Lidda and Mialee would make a move on the guards combining the wizard's magic with the halfling's skill, then all of them would head toward the camp. The rogue would infiltrate the place, locate the staff, and remove it from under the gnolls' noses.

Lidda had to rely on Mialee's sight until she was close enough to the gnolls to act on her own. The wizard was not slowed by the darkness so much as the halfling. Her eyes were able to see much farther than Lidda's under the indistinct light of the moon and stars. It was a gift of her elf blood and a trait that she and Vadania shared.

"Remember that the gnolls' night vision surpasses even your own," the druid said to Mialee as she dropped to her knees, signaling for the others to do the same.

Malthooz squatted next to Krusk. Dampness soaked through his breeches as he knelt in the bushes. It was getting cold again, and the wetness only added to his discomfort. He felt like he'd been soaked for days.

The darkness of the forest closed in around them as twilight faded into night. It was oddly reassuring to Malthooz the way the shadows smothered all the details of his surroundings, allowing him to convince himself that he was somewhere else. He wasn't sure, but he felt that he was better off not being able to see more clearly in the gloom, not knowing who or what was out there. Maybe it was Krusk's presence that calmed his nerves. He fingered the symbol of Pelor through his shirt while watching Vadania and Krusk kneeling nearby. He wondered if the disk would offer him any protection in the worst case or if it would do anything at all.

Malthooz saw Krusk look over at him. The barbarian sneered, but Malthooz didn't feel it was directed at him so much as at something more general.

"This is all I need," the barbarian said, showing Malthooz the butt of his axe. He spat. "Not that it's going to see any use tonight."

Krusk glared at Mialee and Lidda as they moved off.

"It'll be easier this way," the druid said.

"Easier for who?" Krusk growled.

Malthooz saw the beauty in the simplicity of the rogue's plan, particularly because it didn't involve a fight. Under the cover of darkness and silence, Lidda would save them all a lot of potential trouble. The idea sounded good to Malthooz, if a bit risky. The only other option was to go straight in and take the thing by force. That was Krusk's preference. Malthooz hoped that there were no more gnolls in the woods.

"I hope she doesn't run into whatever left the other set of footprints," Vadania said as Mialee and Lidda slipped from sight.

Krusk cracked his knuckles and said, "We'll know soon enough."

Malthooz had forgotten about the other prints.

"Twelve, thirteen, fourteen . . ."

Lidda crept silently across the soft earth, counting to herself under her breath. She circled slowly around the guards, keeping them just in sight as she moved from tree to tree. The gnolls were sharing drinks between themselves. The rogue didn't need to guess at its nature. One of the creatures wiped a long arm across its muzzle as it fell back against a tree and passed a ceramic urn to its partner.

They resembled nothing so much as bipedal wolves. They were roughly humanoid and stood about the same height as Krusk. Matted fur, dark gray with the white sheen of their winter coats, covered their bodies from head to foot. Patches of hair showed through the joints in their armor. Toughened plates of leather covered their shoulders, chests, and thighs. The pieces were held in place with a network of cords and buckles. Their snouts ended in black, canine noses. Sharp teeth lined their elongated jaws.

A pair of longbows rested on a stump nearby, next to bundles of arrows. Each of the creatures had a sword strapped to its side.

". . . forty-nine, fifty."

Lidda finished her count and moved around the tree, praying that she and Mialee had their timing right. As if on cue, a shimmering wall of color materialized in the air in front of the drunken gnolls. One of them shook its head as it tried to figure out what it was seeing. It reached out to touch the shimmering pattern of light dancing before its eyes, whimpering as it pawed at nothingness.

Before it had time to react, Lidda's dagger found the addled guard's throat. A second later, it was on the ground choking on its own blood, the urn still clutched in its paw. The gnoll's companion was so enrapt in the spell, it didn't even see the first victim fall. Lidda drew her dagger across the throat of the second gnoll and it slumped to the earth.

Her weapon was wiped clean and in its sheath by the time Mialee reached her. Lidda checked through the bodies as Mialee stood watch. She rummaged through the creature's armor but turned up only a few silver coins. She dropped them into a pouch at her belt. Grabbing the jug that the gnolls had been drinking from, she took a sniff of the contents.

"Strong drink," the rogue said passing it to Mialee. "A few more pulls and I wouldn't have needed my knife."

The wizard tossed the mug aside. "No thanks," she said. "Let's get back to the others. We have more to do."

"The easy part's done," Lidda said minutes later as she and Mialee huddled down beside Vadania and the half-orcs. She upended her pouch of coins on the dirt in front Malthooz's feet. "Bonus pay," she said grinning. "Take 'em for luck."

Malthooz reached for the coins but pulled his hand back when he saw the dried blood covering them.

Krusk snorted. "I better see more than that," he said. "All of this work and I haven't even seen a proper fight."

"No offense," Mialee said, "but if we're getting paid either way, I'll take the easy gold."

Vadania got up, saying, "We should move. I'd like to get this job done and get out of the woods by morning. We'll have the whole camp on our tail when they figure out what we've done. The farther away we are when that happens, the better."

They moved along under the light of the moon that was riding full in the sky. The yellow glow of its half crescent made it easier to see the land around them and they were not so dependant of the elf women for sight. Lidda moved in the front of the group with Mialee and Vadania. They conferred in hushed tones, going over their plans a final time as they approached the outskirts of the camp.

Vadania kneeled in the bushes at the edge of the clearing that the gnolls' camp occupied. She pointed at a large tent standing at the center of the outpost.

"That's the one," she said. "If I had to wager, I'd say the staff's in there."

Lidda nodded. Fifty yards stretched between her and the rear of the tent. She studied the area, memorizing the details, making mental notes as she considered her task. A number of smaller tents were spaced around the clearing at odd intervals. Crude cloth, stitched together pieces of animal skins and patches of gaudily colored cloth, covered the structures. They were circular in shape, their coverings suspended on wooden frames that radiated out from tall central poles. Off to one side sat a sagging, wooden building. It looked like an old logging shack and gave the whole area a dilapidated feel. The rogue calculated the distance between buildings, noting where each of them was. She wanted to know where to expect trouble to come from and where enemy eyes might lurk.

A company of gnolls was seated around a fire blazing near the circle of tents. The creatures passed two jugs among themselves. Lidda smiled to herself—they would be even easier to get past than the sentries, she thought, judging by the length of their drinks and their loud, slurred speech that echoed through the surrounding woods.

Lidda wrinkled her nose. "The whole area reeks of wet dog," she said.

Krusk crept up to the druid's side.

"I count six," he said. "How many more did you see?"

Vadania replied, "I didn't want to get too close. I'd say there are at least that many in the camp proper, and that many again around here somewhere."

"Probably passed out," Malthooz said.

"And no sign of the other?" Lidda asked, an image of Krusk's boot inside the huge prints in her head. "This should be easy."

"Drunk or not, these are savage fighters, Lidda," Krusk corrected. "Remember the plan. In and out. Find the wizard's stick and be done with it."

Mialee grinned at the barbarian and said, "I thought you hated the plan."

"If it's got to go this way, I'd just as soon be done with it," he growled. "The sooner we're done with the thieves guild, the better."

"Funny that the gnolls weren't so big and fierce a few minutes ago when you were ready to waltz in by yourself," the rogue said, winking at the barbarian.

Krusk snorted.

"The rest of us will fan out," Mialee said. "Vadania and I can cover you with bows and slings if need be. Krusk and Malthooz can move in close in case things get hairy. Remember that there might be other guards."

"Check," the rogue said, raising the hood of her cloak.

She slipped off toward the camp, a shadow among shadows, and crept around behind the largest of the tents, keeping herself pressed low to the ground. She felt the warm burn of her thigh muscles tensing as she concentrated on her movement. It was good to be alone. She breathed in the night air. It wasn't that she didn't like her companions. She just needed some space to herself once in a while. Especially when she was facing a task like the present one, she liked to work solo.

She thought about what an association with the guild might mean for her. It would be as official a recognition of her skills as she could hope for. She would still be operating in gray areas as far as the law was concerned, but she'd be able to leave behind the petty theft and pickpocketing. Her work would gain official sanction, for lack of a better way to put it. At least among certain circles, that is. New contacts within the underground network in Newcoast alone would be worth the hardship. She wasn't sure that her companions would see it the same way. She knew how Krusk felt about it, anyway.

The large tent stood a few yards from where she was. The distance was not too great, and the remaining guards had their backs turned to her. Lidda covered the distance to the main tent in three quick steps. The mass of the pavilion separated her from the gnolls still drinking around the fire. Lidda pressed herself against the rough surface of the tent, feeling its uneven surface brush the side of her cheek. She put her ear to the canvas but heard nothing. Not a sound emerged from inside. She took a deep breath, letting the sweet, pine scent of the forest calm her. She glanced back to her companions and made her move.

Dropping to the ground alongside the tent, she lifted the edge of the cover and peered inside. The interior was almost black, and it took a few moments for the rogue's eyes to adjust to the darkness. A dim glow streamed through an opening in the ceiling. It must have functioned as a chimney of sorts, she thought. Red coals glowed in the fire pit in the center of the room, but the flames of the blaze had long since gone out. Slowly, she began to make out more of the details of the space.

From her vantage point, Lidda could discern the shape of a gnoll sleeping atop a crude cot. A table and chair sat on the far side of the room, remnants of the gnoll's last meal littering the surface. A chalice lay on its side next to the scraps of food, its contents nothing more than a dark puddle on the floor. A large wooden chest sat just to the side of the creature's bed. She studied the bands of reinforcing steel that ringed the trunk. Lidda would wager her share of the take that whatever was inside was what she was after.

She paused. Something about the room bothered her. Something about it didn't make sense. The gnolls didn't seem settled enough to be permanent residents at the camp, but the tent was too well equipped to be the home of a nomad. She was overanalyzing, she told herself. Lidda pushed her doubts aside. She was there for one reason and one reason alone.

She crawled into the tent and moved past the sleeping gnoll toward the chest. She would normally have slit the monster's throat. Something held her back, though. It would have been an easy kill. Was it the thought of being caught by the creature's companions outside that held her back, she wondered? She shook her head. That wasn't it. It was almost as though she felt Eva Flint scrutinizing her every move and had to prove to the guild master that she could pull off the heist without resorting to her dagger. Lidda stopped herself. She was letting her ego get the better of her work. She paused for a moment to regain her concentration before she crawled the final few feet.

The chest didn't look like anything special. The lock appeared simple enough. Lidda pulled a slender steel wire from inside her cloak and inserted it into the opening on the front of the trunk. She jiggled the tool carefully, feeling for the telltale sign of a trapping mechanism. The thin steel wire acted as an extension of her fingers. Years of training and practice allowed the halfling to interpret the subtle messages she felt through the instrument. She could feel the workings of the lock but felt no other triggers or catches. She removed the tool, satisfied that the mechanism was clean.

Lidda pulled a more substantial utensil from her cloak. The pick looked like a key but was larger, with multiple nodules and bumps running the length of its shaft. Lidda worked it back and forth slowly inside the lock, feeling a slight bounce as each of the mechanism's cams dropped into place. One after another, she worked them into the proper grooves. As the last one was finessed into place, the lock opened with a click. Lidda slid a clasp from the loop of steel holding the latch of the chest closed and raised the lid slightly.

Deep within sat a wooden box that was just under three feet long. Its surface was dark brown with thick lines of growth showing in the grain. It had been sanded smooth. The innate markings in the wood were accented with silver paint, turning its natural imagery into something entirely different. Demonic faces stared at Lidda from the top of the box, glowing in the pale light that filtered through the top of the tent. The images shimmered and changed as she watched them. The faces became dragons and the dragons became the faces of people she'd known. Tiny spiders, their legs as thin as thread, danced across the surface as ocean waves lapped along the edges of the box. Mountains rose and fell. Time seemed to stop, and to accelerate, all at once.

Lidda shook her head. What kind of trickery is this? she thought.

She looked around the room, unsure how long she'd been held in thrall by the phantasms in the trunk. The gnoll slept on its cot, snoring quietly, and the embers in the fire pit still glowed a dull orange-red. She had been staring for only a few minutes at most.

As her hand hit the top of the thing, the swirling patterns stopped. Curious, she thought, as she lifted the box gingerly from the bottom of the chest. It was not as heavy as she expected it to be. The wood alone should have weighed several pounds, yet the whole thing was as light as a single crossbow bolt. Everything about the item was wondrous. The rogue couldn't imagine the worth of the container, let alone what rested inside. She cleared the lid of the trunk and turned to go.

As she moved away, a single, clear chime sounded. It was not loud, but in the silence of the tent it was a clamor. Lidda jumped to her feet. She noticed a small piece of delicate string running from the bottom of the treasure to a silver bell suspended in a corner of the trunk.

"Damn," she cursed her own stupidity under her breath.

On guard for a much more ingenious or perhaps magical trap, she'd been betrayed by this simple and elegant mechanism. She heard the gnoll stirring behind her. Holding her prize under her arm, she darted for the entrance flap.

Krusk saw Lidda emerge from the flap of the tent in a sprint. She frantically scanned the camp. A howl went up from within the canvas shelter, where Lidda had just been. The barbarian knew that trouble was on the way.

He hefted his axe. The heady rush of a good fight would be welcome. He looked back at Mialee and Vadania. The women were startled by the sudden sound of the gnoll's yell. Malthooz stood up beside Krusk. His eyes were wide. He held the quarterstaff in his hand but tossed it aside and grabbed the club from his belt. The symbol of Pelor dangled exposed from the cord around his neck.

Krusk whistled to Lidda, and she started toward the bushes where the half-orcs were hiding.

He turned to Malthooz and whispered, "Now you'll get your first taste of battle. Keep close to the halfling, and remember what I taught you."

He heard Malthooz offering up a hushed prayer.

A gnoll near the fire toppled over with an arrow sticking from its chest. Another reeled back as a stone from Vadania's sling caught it in the side of the head. Krusk felt his blood rise. He wasn't going to let the elf women show him up. The frustration of the past few days boiled in his veins, and he was going to make someone pay.

Lidda reached the barbarian's side as the camp erupted.

"There was a trap," she cursed. "I was careless."

"That doesn't matter now," Krusk said, stepping toward the camp. "Keep an eye on Malthooz."

The barbarian let out a roar and charged into the clearing.

A small, elite band of gnolls reacted to their commander's alarm immediately. They slipped from the tent nearest his, heavily armored and well armed, and fanned themselves across the campsite. Breaking into three groups, they took positions of cover around the scene. Each of them carried a longbow on its shoulder and had a cruelly curved sword at its hip. One of them sneered at its drunken pack mates, lashing out with its foot. The stricken soldier scrambled across the ground looking for its weapon.

Their commander, Yauktul, had long ago learned the usefulness of allowing his men to let off steam. He held his tongue as they drank themselves into a stupor, realizing that they would do it behind his back if he did not allow them the pleasure. He was tired of the work it took to keep all of his warriors in line, yet he realized the importance of having a solid core of loyal guards who would faithfully obey him at all times and who did not indulge in the foul drink enjoyed by their brethren. These dedicated guards were rewarded for their service, though their payment was kept quiet from the others to avoid unnecessary tension or outright mutiny.

The elite warriors appraised the situation, their superior night vision allowing them to take in everything. As one, they took the longbows from their shoulders and trained them on the startled intruders.

"Damn."

Mialee heard Vadania's curse as she spotted the gnolls with their bows trained on them. The wizard dropped to her knees and began casting a spell that would ward herself from attack. A barrier sprang into place in front of the women as she spoke the final words of magic.

Mialee reached for her bow as an arrow bounced harmlessly off the magic shield. She saw Vadania loose a bullet from her sling as a second arrow flew past the druid, within inches of her head.

"Cover me," Vadania hissed as she let go of her sling and began casting a spell of her own.

Mialee fired with abandon, more interested in keeping the gnolls off guard than in scoring a hit. She fired time and again, raining a rapid barrage of arrows on the creatures. Gnolls scattered for cover as the hail of arrows whistled and clattered all around them.

Mialee heard the familiar scrape of a blade being drawn as Vadania stepped forth, brandishing the scimitar that she favored for close combat. In the center of the camp, a pair of wolves appeared. They burst into a tangle of gnolls, tearing through the creatures with their fangs.

Vadania ran toward the camp. "Lets go," she hollered, "the wolves are a strong distraction, but they won't last long."

She raised her weapon and charged into the fray.

Mialee fired a volley of magical bolts at the nearest gnoll. The glowing spears burned through the creature's thick fur and bit the soft flesh beneath. She watched as Vadania advanced, distracting a gnoll with a jet of flame from her palm before catching it across the cheek with her sword. The creature fell back, caught between its fear of magic and the harsh reality of steel. Vadania grabbed its arm as it turned, sending the blazing fire up its length. The gnoll fell to the ground screaming as its fur burst into flame.

Mialee plunged into the battle, loosing another round of magical spears as she went.

Malthooz heard the dull thud of arrows striking trees. He leaped to the side as one grazed past his ear. All around him he heard the buzz of missiles passing through the air.

"You'll be cut to shreds up there," Lidda said.

She grabbed his leg and yanked him down.

This was not at all what he expected. Things were happening too fast for him to deal with. He watched Krusk sprint from the edge of the forest. The barbarian moved directly on the closest pair of gnolls. The monsters dropped their bows and drew long swords as he rushed them, but before the blades could clear their sheaths, Krusk was upon them. The first gnoll went down soundlessly, sliced nearly in half at the waist. The second, having a moment more to react, squared off with Krusk, its sword raised against the barbarian's blows.

The woods filled with the sound of combat. The clash of steel on steel rang in Malthooz's ears as more arrows sailed over him. He held his club at his side. Sweat from his palm made the weapon hard to grasp. Beside him, Lidda was training her crossbow on the melee. Malthooz searched the woods for more danger. Shadows from the trees seemed to move and shift, taking on the appearance of moving foes.

Back in the clearing, Krusk and the gnoll were locked in combat. Malthooz watched as the two shifted back and forth. He winced as he watched the monster's sword cut a gash in the barbarian's leg.

Mialee and Vadania joined Krusk, moving into view from their spot at the edge of the clearing. Malthooz's head spun with the fury of the scene. It was hard for the half-orc to tell his companions from his enemies. He had no idea where to begin.

Lidda dropped her crossbow. "I can't risk a shot," she said, drawing the short sword from her side. "We've got to move in." She crept up. "Stay close to me."

Malthooz gulped and followed her into the fray. They moved along the ground toward the center of the camp. Krusk was still tangling with his opponent as more gnolls emerged from their tents around the clearing. They looked disoriented at first, but they snapped out of their stupor when they spotted the barbarian in their midst and saw Malthooz and Lidda approaching.

Before he knew what he was doing, Malthooz found himself in the middle of the fight. He moved with Lidda as the rogue cut a path through the gnolls toward Krusk. Malthooz let out a groan when a gnoll appeared in the space between him and the rogue. He swung his club at the thing's nose, catching the tip of it and sending the creature yelping into Lidda's back. The rogue spun on the beast and plunged her sword into its chest.

"Careful," she hissed.

Malthooz and the halfling fought side by side, the rogue's sword slashing through the ranks of gnolls as the half-orc brought his club to bear. Another gnoll fell to the ground, clutching its broken wrist where Malthooz's club had struck. Malthooz felt the frenzy of combat pounding in his head. The pulse of blood rushing through his ears drowned out the sounds of the fighting going on all around him. He swung his club at anything that moved, whether it was in reach or not. He felt it smash in the side of a skull with a sickening sound.

The halfling and the half-orc worked well together in a strange sort of way, the rogue keeping her body between Malthooz and gnoll's blades while he swung his club at them over her head. It was an awkward but effective tactic. His unseasoned recklessness kept the creature's guard up while the rogue's sword found its purchase in their flesh. The rest of the company fought alongside them. The bodies of dead gnolls littered the ground at their feet as the companions slashed through the monsters' ranks.

The crunch of heavy footsteps sounded in the woods nearby, coming over the more immediate noise of fighting, echoing above the ringing in the half-orc's' ears. Malthooz turned on the commotion in time to see the huge form of an ettin erupt into the camp. A harsh and dissonant screech peeled through the air as the giant rushed forward, covering the length of a body with each of its tremendous strides. Malthooz shouted an incoherent warning.

Two sets of eyes fell on the half-orc, whose knees trembled at the sight of the thing. It was a grotesque monster, unlike anything he'd ever imagined. Two heads sat upon massive shoulders. Each face was riddled with warts and scabs. Rotten brown teeth protruded from the creature's lower jaws. Its legs and arms were the size of small oaks. Either of its hands was easily as big as the half-orc's head. Thin, greasy hair hung limp over the creature's brows. It was clothed in a crude, hide loincloth. Bits of dried flesh still clung to the garment.

Mialee turned on the ettin with her magic bolts. A trio of them raced from her fingertips at the giant. The missiles slammed into the creature, burning holes in its thick clothing but doing little else.

The gnolls backed off as the giant waded into the melee wielding the lower half of a tree as a weapon. It moved toward Krusk at once, bringing the huge club around on the barbarian, sending him reeling to the side to avoid the blow. The return swing caught both of Vadania's phantasmal wolves, sending their broken bodies hurtling across the camp.

The ettin's attacks became less precise as the passion of the fight overtook it. It leveled a handful of fleeing gnolls, catching them on the end of its tree as they tried to get away from the flailing stump. The rest of the gnolls backed off entirely to the edge of the clearing, not wanting to run but unwilling to stay within the ettin's indiscriminate reach.

Malthooz blinked as he watched Mialee disappear for an instant then reappear at the ettin's side. The wizard flashed into and out of sight while she struck at the creature's feet with her staff.

The door flap of the main tent was thrown open from inside. A large gnoll stood in the doorway, mumbling words, its hands weaving patterns in the air. Malthooz felt something rubbing against his boots. He tried to lift his foot but it was held firmly to the ground. The earth seemed to come alive under his feet as tiny sprouts sprang up around him, snaking their way up his legs. The vines wrapped themselves up his calf, tightening as they grew.

He looked around at the others. All of them were caught in a web of foliage. Its spell completed, the gnoll dashed from the tent and into the woods.

"He's mine," Lidda said, hacking at the ground with her sword. She severed the last of the creepers that held her in place and raced after the fleeing gnoll.

Krusk and Mialee faced the giant, all three of them literally rooted to the battle. As it bent to add leverage to its swing, the barbarian's axe flashed upward and severed one of the ettin's heads from the body. Like an enormous melon, it rolled across the clearing, leaving behind a splashed trail of blood. One hand slipped from the giant's club as it lost control of half of its body. The beast spun in a circle, one leg tangled in foliage, the other stomping free, as it swung the tree around. Mialee dodged to the side and slammed her staff into the creature's chin. With a loud pop, the weapon snapped in two, but the jagged end stabbed upward through the ettin's jaw. The giant toppled backward, crashing into the side of a tent and bringing the structure flapping down around itself.

Seeing their champion down, the gnolls watching from the edges of the clearing turned and scattered into the gloom of the forest, leaving their attackers in possession of the camp.

"I lost the spellcaster," Lidda wheezed, her breath coming in short rapid breaths. "At least we have the staff. And I found this in its tent."

She tossed a roll of heavy parchment to Mialee. The wizard grabbed the thing, unfurling it and studying the writing on its surface. Arcane symbols covered its length. The wizard stuffed it into her pouch.

Lidda squatted down and set the box on the ground.

"It makes no sense to me that a band of gnolls would be after this magical device," she said, running her hand along the smooth surface of the case. The ornate silver lines that were previously animated still traced the natural contours of the wood but no longer moved as they had.

Vadania unwrapped a length of vine from her boot and threw it aside.

"It makes little difference now," she said. "We have what we were after."

"And I doubt the others will be back," Mialee said, "with the giant dead and their leader gone."

"That's probably true," the druid agreed. "Still, I'll feel better when we've put more ground between ourselves and this place."

"I agree," Malthooz said.

He touched the druid's arm. A warmth passed over his hand and into Vadania's body through the tips of his fingers. Vadania pulled away from him. Scrapes on her legs from the entanglement quickly healed over.

Malthooz stared in amazement, then touched the symbol hanging from his neck. It felt like a lifeless piece of wood. He felt no different from before, but all of them saw what happened.

Vadania ran her hand over her skin.

"Perhaps you were visited by Pelor after all, Malthooz," she said.

"Stick to the club," Krusk snarled, and moved away to search the bodies of the fallen gnolls.

Vadania ignored the barbarian's comment.

"Now maybe you'll take some time to find out," she said.

They searched the area hastily. Krusk found a pile of torches in one of the tents and Malthooz watched the cone of flame moving through the darkness as the barbarian passed among the bodies of the dead gnolls. Lidda and Mialee combed through the wooden building. Malthooz and Vadania stood guard near the wizard's box.

Malthooz tried to look calm, but he quietly berated himself. He hadn't done a thing during the fight. The magic, if that's what it was, moved through him without warning, unannounced and actually unwelcome. He wasn't sure what he expected, carrying the holy symbol with him on a cord around his neck. He'd seen the women use their magic many times, but it was under their control, arising intentionally. Even the shaman from the village worked with the utmost attention, whether or not what he did was truly magical. What was happening to him? None of the others seemed very concerned.

Malthooz knew that they were accustomed to the unusual, used to not relying on assumptions to get them through. They certainly didn't trust their lives to something they didn't understand. Not even Krusk appeared overly alarmed by what he'd seen, even if his distaste was obvious.

Malthooz heard Vadania approach.

"It sounds like the gnolls have regrouped and are returning," she said.

Newcoast bustled with activity as Lidda moved through the streets toward the Bung and Blade. She passed the rows of ships at harbor and the wharves that lined the waterfront. Stout and long merchant vessels rocked gently in their berths as workers unloaded cargo using a simple system of pulleys and booms. Many more ships had left the previous day, taking advantage of the mild weather, hoping to make it to the next port before another storm hit. A few more arrived in the port earlier that morning, setting the docks in motion.

From the gnolls' camp, they reached the city in three days by traveling hard. They headed south, straight through the forest. Low clouds followed them for most of the trip, hovering just above the tops of the trees. The weather followed them right into town. The air was thick and damp everywhere, inside and out, though it didn't rain. At least the blanket of haze brought relief from the bitter cold. The trip had been thankfully free from serious pursuit and uneventful.

Merchants' carts lined the streets and people of every description jostled amongst them, haggling over prices and quality. Lidda stopped to admire the assortment of daggers that one man was selling, with her eyes on a set of jeweled throwing blades. She waved the peddler off and moved down the row of vendors. She had no idea what use one would have for such weapons, but when she returned to the guild the next morning, she'd walk away with enough gold to buy all of them and more, if she had the mind to. She walked into the pub and found her friends sitting at a table in the rear.

"I've set a meeting with Flint and Wotherwill for tomorrow morning," she said, grinning from ear to ear. She put her elbow into Krusk's ribs. "You'll get your payment yet, and you got your fight."

Krusk grunted.

"Malthooz has been at him again," Vadania explained.

Lidda clicked her tongue against the roof of her mouth.

"I'm going to leave after we get paid," he said. "At least Krusk thinks I did enough to earn my share."

Lidda smiled at the half-orc and said, "You saved my hide."

"Still playing with that thing?" Lidda asked, seeing Malthooz's trinket on the table in front of him.

Vadania grabbed the symbol from the table.

"I think I've talked him into learning more," she said. "We all saw what he did to my wounds."

Malthooz looked down at the table.

Lidda was going to miss the half-orc. She'd grown fond of him, as had the other women. He was awkward and too modest, but the rogue liked him. She grabbed his hand.

"You know you're always welcome, anywhere you can find us. That goes for this oaf, too." She elbowed Krusk again. "Speaking of oafs—you still got the staff?"

Krusk set his hand on the bench beside him.

"It's not leaving my sight until you take it back to the old man," he said. "I won't trust him or the thieves guild until I've got some gold in my hand and twenty miles between me and this city."

Lidda left early the next morning, leaving the rest of the company at the inn. She carried the box containing the staff under her arm, wrapped in cloth to avoid drawing attention.

Krusk thought it made no sense that the gnolls were acting alone, and he found it hard to believe that the creatures just stumbled upon the ship while they had a giant in tow. He'd been griping about it all night, weaving his inborn skepticism into a web of conspiracy and deceit.

Lidda had to admit that they never got much of a story from Wotherwill, and what they did hear they'd accepted almost entirely without questioning. She wasn't too worried about the half-orc's suspicions, though. The way she saw it, the staff had probably been in the hands of the gnolls to begin with and the creatures had simply been reclaiming it. Either way, the business would be done soon, or at least her part would be. She couldn't care less where the thing came from. She'd feel no regret for taking it from the gnolls even if it was theirs. The weight of the container felt good under her arm as she tried to calculate the staff's weight in gold. Krusk's worries were over nothing.

She rounded a corner and moved onto the lane that ran behind the guild. It was wider than most of the alleyways in the city but wasn't' quite a street. There were a number of small windows in the wall, and the detailed trim motif on the front of the building continued around through the rear. A few boarded-up doorways lined the other side of the alley.

Lidda felt along the wall, searching for the small catch that would open a panel in the surface. Flint had told her about the alternate entrance the previous afternoon. Lidda took it as yet another sign that she was gaining the guild master's favor. She glanced over her shoulder to make sure no one was watching then slid open a concealed door.

After stepping quickly into a small passageway, Lidda

pushed the wall closed behind her. The short, dark, narrow hallway inside the wall ended a dozen paces ahead. She guessed that her entrance was being watched.

At the far wall, she rapped the way Flint had indicated. A moment later a second panel slid open and the rogue found herself facing the doorman she met on her first visit. He nodded at the halfling, then his eyes shifted to the bulk under her arm. He turned without a word and led her through the complex to the guild master's chamber.

Eva Flint was seated behind her desk. She smiled as the rogue entered the room. Wotherwill sat at a chair at her side, fidgeting with the hem of his robes. Lidda walked boldly into the room and set the bundle in front of them. The old wizard held the key in his hand, rubbing the top of the dragon's head with his long fingers.

Wotherwill leaned forward in his chair. A hunger came over his eyes as he reached for the box.

"Ah," he sighed, "a lifetime of work reaches its climax. This treasure cost me two wives and the loss of my only child." He lifted the box from the desktop. "Grievous losses each, in their own way, but this," he said, running a bony finger along its surface, "makes them bearable."

He reached a shaky hand toward the clasp on the front of the box. The black figurine of the dragon shifted as it was brought close to the lock. Minute, ebony wings unfolded as though the creature was about to take flight. The statue's slender neck extended to meet the clasp. Shifting silvery lines animated themselves on the surface of the wood as if the two artifacts longed for each other.

Wotherwill inserted the key into an opening in the front of the wooden box. The dancing patterns on the surface of the container suddenly stopped their illusionary movement, aligning themselves into a geometric grid. With a click, the lid of the chest sprang open.

A soft glow from the interior of the box fell across the wizard's face and he lifted the staff from within. The artifact was magnificent, beyond anything Lidda had ever seen. Even without magical properties, the item would have been priceless. A thin wire of gold was sunk into the shaft, winding its way up the staff to the crown, where it flowered into a blossom of diamonds and opals. The staff grew as Wotherwill lifted it free of its confines until it was twice its original length. The top of the thing radiated a diffused, green glow.

Eva Flint rose from her seat and said, "You seem pleased, wizard."

"Quite, m'lady. Quite pleased indeed." Wotherwill's gaze didn't stray from the staff as he nodded. He ran a hand down the length of the shaft. "Quite pleased indeed."

He lowered the staff back toward the box. As it neared the container, the staff shrank to accommodate its housing. Wotherwill reached for a sack that lay on the floor near his chair.

"You will find the agreed upon amount inside," he said, handing the pouch to Lidda, "plus a little extra for your troubles. Lady Flint told me of the bandits."

Lidda opened the sack and peered inside. A mound of gold with a few modest-sized gems mixed in rested at the bottom.

"I trust there's no need to count this here," she said, casting Flint a glance as she sealed the bag, "and that the guild has already seen its cut?"

Flint nodded.

"Then it is settled," Wotherwill said, bowing to each of the women. "I'll take my leave now."

Flint summoned the doorman, and the wizard was shown from the chamber. Lidda hesitated a moment, unsure how to proceed. She turned to leave.

"I guess I'll be going, too," she said, moving for the door.

"Wait one minute," Flint commanded, taking her seat. "I'd like to hear more about these *bandits*." The final word rang thick with sarcasm. "I like to keep tabs on those who might try to move in on my territory."

"Just a band of gnolls, as far as I could tell," Lidda said. "They had a two-headed giant with them, but I suppose that's not too strange. It's not with them anymore."

"Not strange at all," Flint said. "I've been dealing with them for a few months now." She leaned back in her chair. "The cretins are trying to muscle in on my shipping interests."

The guild master summoned the doorman and had Lidda shown to the door. Lidda turned to bow to Flint as she left, thinking it would only get her wedged even more deeply into the woman's good graces. As she raised her eyes from the floor, she caught the quick flash of Flint's hands, the subtle movement of her fingers.

Good work, she signalled, *I'll be in touch.*

Eva Flint pushed her chair back, tipping it up on two legs and setting her boots on the desk. She slid a dagger from under the seat and was carelessly running her finger along the blade as Yauktul was shown into the room. She motioned the commander to a seat with a flick of the blade. The gnoll looked nervously over his shoulders, at both Flint and the departing doorman, as he moved across the room. When the door clicked behind the doorman, Yauktul fell to his knees.

"It was not my fault," he whimpered.

Eva looked at the creature with disgust.

"Get up," she said. "Your presence repulses me, so I would keep this short."

The chair slammed back to the ground as the guild master lunged forward and slammed her blade into the desk. Yauktul yelped and drew back, looking as if he wanted nothing more than to bolt from the room.

Eva got up from her seat and moved around the front of the desk. Yauktul cringed as she brought her hand down on his head to stroke the crest of hair that crowned it. She cooed to the creature as she petted him.

"Yauktul, Yauktul," she tisked.

She grabbed a handful of fur and yanked. The commander's neck snapped back as his eyes were brought into line with hers.

"You failed me," she said, pulling harder on the creature's fur, craning his neck farther.

Yauktul whimpered and Eva let go. The gnoll commander's eyes fell back to the floor. She scrubbed the front of her breeches to wipe the gnoll's musky scent off her hand.

Pitiful, she thought, that such a being would be considered a leader among its own kind.

It had a small aptitude for the art of magic, and she'd interpreted that as a sign of intelligence. She never should have trusted the damned thing, but she had too much time, gold, and effort invested in this undertaking to watch the treasure slip from her grasp. She had to make one last effort.

"You can still make it up to me," Flint said, stroking the gnoll's head again.

The guild master walked back to her desk and leaned against it.

"You," she said, turning back to Yauktul, "know what you have to do."

She lifted the dagger from the desk and hurled it to the floor near the gnoll's clawed foot. Yauktul jumped back when the tip of the blade struck and clattered across the stone floor.

"This time, failure is not an option if you value your life. Now get out of my sight."

The gnoll rushed to the door and disappeared into the

hallway. Eva returned to her seat. She lowered herself into the chair slowly, calmly, then slammed her fist on the desk. It would be impossible to keep the city's officials away from this. Wotherwill only pretended to be a hermit, she knew. He was well connected within the circles of the city's gentry. His political ties alone outweighed the worth of the staff in her estimation, and they made him more dangerous than his magic, which was considerable. There had always been risk, but more was at stake. Too much more to even consider backing out. Whatever Wotherwill's connections and power, her chief clients were wealthier and better connected than he would ever be. Eva smiled to herself. The rogue and her companions would prove to be of use yet.

It was a pity, she mused. She was starting to like the halfling.

The scene at the Bung and Blade that evening was raucous to say the least. The whole of the company was warm with the intoxication of ale, and even Krusk loosened up after half a dozen rounds. Mialee stopped the barbarian from ordering drinks for the entire waterfront, cringing at the thought of an army of acquired friends.

"We don't need to advertise our fortune to the world," Mialee murmured, looking around the pub.

Dozens of rowdy sailors filled the place from wall to wall. A trio of them stood on a table on the far side of the room trying to rouse the assembled rabble into song. So far, they'd only managed to stir up a handful of glares.

Malthooz was face down on the table. It hadn't taken much to put him under. Mialee felt bad for the half-orc. He tried to match the rest of the company and it wasn't long before he was talking wildly about his plans to bring his powers back to the village and replace the shaman with a new order of healers, with him at the head. Krusk egged him on as probably only he could have, though the wizard believed it had less to do with spite or jest than with the empty tankards piled high in front of the barbarian. Krusk had also convinced Malthooz that heavy drinking was his birthright, something required by his blood. The more they drank, the louder they became, until Malthooz collapsed in mid-bellow. Even the sailors were beginning to get exasperated by the time Malthooz passed out. Vadania did her best to hide the unconscious half-orc behind her backpack.

As the night wore on, the mood grew more sour.

"I wish I had slit that gnoll's throat when I had the chance," Lidda said, stuffing her mouth full of fried potatoes. "Flint said there's a bounty on them. She says the city pays fifty gold a head."

Krusk looked up from his plate and growled, "I told you from the start that we shouldn't get ourselves mixed up with the thieves guild." He pushed his plate away. "Those cutthroats have no regard for anyone but themselves and their own purses."

"Well, they didn't hurt our cause too much," Mialee said.

She had the parchment Lidda found at the camp spread out on the table in front of her, and she was glancing at it between bites.

Krusk grunted, "Suit yourself. I'll have nothing more to do with them."

Vadania glanced down at Mialee's scroll.

"Have you figured out what that does yet?" she asked.

The wizard shook her head and replied, "No, but I will, once I have the chance to really study it." She stuffed it back into a hollow bone tube. "This isn't the place for it, though."

"Suit yourself, yourself, Krusk," Lidda said. "I think I'll be seeing more work from the guild."

Malthooz awoke with a throbbing in his head unlike any he'd ever felt before. It was even sharper than the headache he suffered after his run-in with the crab. He reached down for the symbol of Pelor, hoping it might offer some relief, but the wooden disk did nothing to quell his discomfort. He rolled over and sat up. A ray of sunlight came through the window. When it struck his eyes, another bolt of pain shot through his skull. He must have slept away half the morning. Krusk's bed was empty, and the women were probably up as well.

He tried to remember what happened the previous evening. There were vague recollections of a fight with Krusk, trying to talk the barbarian into going north with him. It hadn't gone well. Malthooz shook his head and pulled on his boots. He wasn't looking forward to leaving, even though he felt that it was time to go. He'd grown to appreciate the others' company. At the beginning of the journey he'd felt like nothing but useless baggage, but since the battle with the gnolls, he felt like he was a part of the group. Still, he had no answers to his important questions, and he was sure that the village needed him, now more than ever. Stiffly, Malthooz got up and made his way to the stairs.

The rooms of the inn were on the second floor of the building. A flight of steps ran from the center of the common room up to a long balcony that overlooked the pub below. Malthooz stumbled to the railing and spotted his friends sitting at a table in the corner. Gripping the handrail tightly, he picked his way carefully to the lower room.

"Rough night?" Lidda asked with a grin as he advanced unsteadily across the floor.

Malthooz grunted, but words were not quick to come. Krusk looked up at him as he took a seat next to Vadania.

"I need to teach you to hold your drink like you hold your club," he said.

Malthooz was relieved that Krusk didn't seem upset over the conversation from the night before. He grinned at the barbarian.

The door opened from outside and three men in armor stepped into the pub. The red crescent moon of the city guard shone on the white tips of their belts and the hilts of their swords. Malthooz watched as one of the men showed the paper he was holding to the man tending the counter. The guard said something to the man and he paused for a moment, then nodded at the companions' table.

Lidda reached under the table toward her leg as the guards made their way across the room. The few other patrons in the bar moved aside to let the men pass. Krusk caught the rogue's movement in the corner of his eye and spun around.

"You're being placed under arrest for the murder of Horace Wotherwill," the guard said, laying the document on the table in front of them.

Pressed into a patch of red wax in the bottom corner of the parchment was the official seal of the mayor of the city.

"Found in a gutter this morning," he said. "Not that it would come as any surprise to you. We've got more than enough witnesses."

"Impossible," Krusk bellowed, slamming his fist on the table and rising from his chair. "We haven't left this inn since yesterday."

The barbarian reached across his body and grabbed the dagger that was strapped to his forearm.

"Don't try anything stu—"

The man's words were cut short when Krusk toppled the table and bowled into him. Plates and mugs sailed through the air, and the barbarian jumped on the man. Krusk's dagger thrust toward the guard's neck, but the man knocked it away with his sword. The shorter blade flew from the barbarian's hand just before the two of them tumbled across the floor.

The rest of the company was on their feet instantly. Other guards with weapons drawn stepped up to threaten Mialee and Vadania, should either of them begin casting a spell. Neither of the women were armed. Ringed by blades, they put up their hands and stood quietly.

As the guards' attention turned to the brawl on the floor, Malthooz lunged from his chair and shot right between the guards and the two women, headed for the front door. He heard the innkeeper shouting as he leaped over the upturned table. The half-orc reached for his club but it wasn't at his side. Three more guards charged into the room, blocking the front entrance. Krusk and the guard officer were rolling across the floor, rabidly pummeling and choking one another. More guards piled onto the fray, trying to separate the two wrestlers, straining to release Krusk's hold on the guard's throat.

With his exit blocked, Malthooz hesitated, but only for a moment. A small hand grasped his robe and pulled him with surprising strength toward the stairs.

"Follow me out of this death trap," he heard Lidda say. "All we can do is save ourselves."

Malthooz looked back at his helpless companions, but he stumbled along in the halfling's wake.

They sprinted up the staircase and across the open hallway. Malthooz paused before the door to his room, intending to retrieve his pack, but the rogue shoved him hard from behind. He glimpsed Krusk's axe resting under the bed in the corner as the doorway to the room slid past.

"There's no way we could escape with all of it," the rogue blurted as they made their way to the window at the end of the passage.

He saw a bulge in the pocket of her cloak, however, and knew that she at least had her share of the gold.

The sound of booted feet pounded up the staircase behind them. Malthooz patted the symbol around his neck and touched the pouch of gold in his own tunic. That would have to do, he thought. Lidda threw open the window and jumped into a crouch on the sill, then disappeared over the edge.

Malthooz, far larger than the nimble halfling, thrust his head and shoulders through the opening and looked down into the narrow alleyway that ran behind the inn. With his stomach churning and the guards charging up the hallway, he dragged the rest of his body over the sill. The ground rushed up fast, but he managed to twist so his legs were mostly beneath him, and he landed on a heap of old straw from the stables. Lidda was crouched in a shadow nearby. As soon as Malthooz touched the ground, she turned and dashed up the alley. Malthooz struggled to his feet and raced after her, chased only by curses from the window of the inn.

Iron cuffs bit into Krusk's flesh. He growled at the jailer who pushed him along the dank hallway lined with iron-barred cells. Mialee and Vadania marched a few paces ahead. Each of the women was gagged to keep them from using magic. Krusk bit down on the rag stuffing his own mouth. It was there simply to keep him from talking.

"I've heard enough of your abuse," the jailer said as Krusk gnashed his teeth against the gag.

The stench of decay filled the area. Body odor, mold, and smoke from burning torches assailed the barbarian's nostrils as he walked along the row of cells. Most of them were occupied.

The group stopped in front of a cell at the far end of the hallway and waited while the jailer searched for the right key. He was an old and frail man. The half-dozen armed guards following the group ensured his safety.

"This should be it," he said, slipping the key into a rusty

keyhole and turning it with a grating clack. The door to the cell squealed open. Krusk felt a boot in his back propelling him inside.

Damp straw was scattered across the floor of the cell. Aside from a small urn in the back corner, the room was bare. Moisture dripped down the rough, stone walls, feeding small patches of green moss growing on the mortar between the blocks. A single, narrow shaft cut through the stonework, letting in a thin stream of light from the streets above. The pale glow that came through the opening cast a small spot of brightness on the otherwise gray floor.

"Welcome to your new home," a guard said as he guided the company into the cell. "It's not much, but you'll get used to it." He chuckled. "Most of 'em do, eventually." He removed the rags that were tied around Vadania's and Mialee's heads. "You're free to try your magic," he said as stuffed the rags into a pocket in the front of his uniform, "but you won't get too far with it here, what with the wards and all."

He looked Krusk up and down but left his gag in place. The jailer shut the cell door, sealing any hope of escape with a long steel key.

"Bah," Krusk sputtered as Mialee untied his gag and tossed the rag aside. "Damn those thieves! I said from the start they were not to be trusted."

"We don't know who is behind this," Vadania said, rubbing her wrists. "I'm not going to jump to conclusions. Your stunt at the inn could have gotten us all killed."

Krusk growled, "Whatever you decide, it won't get us out of here. Not with the city's officials giving our arrest their backing." He spat. "I don't know who is worse, the thieves or the politicians."

He looked around the cell. Deep scratches marked one of the walls, a series of short lines running in parallel across its length. He tried to count the marks but quickly lost track. He wasn't sure if they were meant to mark days, weeks, or months, but he was determined that, one way or another, he would not spend any length of time behind bars.

"At least Malthooz and Lidda escaped," Mialee said hopefully. "We'll get out of this yet. After all, we're innocent."

Laughter rang up and down the row of cells, and the barbarian joined it.

"Who are you trying to convince, wizard?"

Krusk wasn't sure which was funnier, leaving his life in the hands of his incompetent "brother" Malthooz or placing his trust in the rogue. He detested both options.

Malthooz hurried down the street behind Lidda. They were moving toward the docks. He had no idea where she was going or what the rogue had in mind. His own mind was racing too quickly for him to reason out anything useful.

They hustled on for what seemed to be hours. Up and down the streets of Newcoast they skulked, keeping an eye out for members of the city guard, trying not to draw attention to themselves while ducking into alleys and doorways at the slightest hint of pursuit. At this point, anyone and everyone that Malthooz trusted was behind bars. Everyone but Lidda, he reminded himself. And how much did he really know about her?

His thoughts drifted to the warmth and camaraderie he'd felt in his own village. All that day he missed it terribly and berated himself for ever leaving. The times he spent seated around a fire listening to the elders telling stories, recounting tales of brave heroes who'd been dead for generations, tales of an all but forgotten age—nothing in the world seemed so appealing to him. He shook his head. Those heroic times were long past, and he was a long way from home. If he held any hope of helping his friends he would have to abandon such romantic notions and deal only with reality.

They made their way slowly along the waterfront, passing the rows of wharves that ran the length of the city's bay. Lidda moved as though she knew what she was looking for. Malthooz had a hard time keeping up, he was hungry and cold, and he wasn't sure how the halfling would react to a question even if he could get her to slow down long enough for him to ask something.

Lidda turned toward the edge of the pier. She looked down for a second then dropped over the side. Malthooz ran to the edge and peered over.

The rogue stood on a narrow dock that was sunken between two larger piers. The platform floated on the surface of the bay, anchored in place by a long row of pilings. A ladder ran from the side of the wharf at Malthooz's feet to the tarred planks below. Lidda had obviously taken a quicker way down.

Malthooz climbed deliberately down the ladder, trying to look nonchalant. Lidda crouched amidst a pile of crates and netting. Malthooz dropped down next to her, his heart pounding. He looked around for signs of the city guard, but no one was in sight. A few squat rowboats bobbed gently along the length of the dock. Above him, Malthooz heard the sounds of men unloading the ships that towered on either side of their hiding spot.

"I've got to go to the guild," Lidda said.

Malthooz shook his head slowly, collecting his thoughts. He wasn't sure that was a good idea. Someone had set them up, and the guild was the prime contender for lead suspect. He didn't want to question Lidda's loyalty to himself and the others, but he knew how much she wanted the guild's favor and thought that her desire might be clouding her judgment.

Lidda obviously saw his hesitation.

"I know that the gnolls are responsible for the wizard's death," she explained. "I think that Wotherwill wasn't being straight with us."

Malthooz listened but didn't respond. Lidda's theory could make sense, if the gnolls had known about the treasure and set out to steal it for reasons that weren't clear. He'd seen the hunger in the old man's eyes during their first meeting and knew how well the wizard had paid them for recovering and delivering the staff. Clearly it was very valuable, but Lidda's theory relied on many "ifs." If the murder and theft had been engineerd by the thieves guild, all the pieces fell into place much more readily.

"Remember, Wotherwill said the thing attracted evil," Lidda argued, "and that gnoll was a spellcaster, too. I think the wizard stole the staff from it in the first place and the gnoll was just stealing it back. Or maybe it was working for another owner."

Malthooz stopped shaking his head, but he still wasn't convinced.

"If you have any better ideas, speak up, Malthooz," spat Lidda. "I know what you're thinking. You don't know whether you can trust me. If the guild was behind all this, then I might be part of it."

Malthooz gulped. The accusation sounded so harsh coming from her.

"If you want to see the others again, we're going to have to work fast, and we're going to have to work together. Once the system in this town gets hold of them, they'll either be put to death or left to rot."

Lidda paused, looking for some sign of agreement from the half-orc, but he only sat silently, head bowed.

"Flint's our only option, whether you trust her or not. She trusted me with this job," the rogue pleaded. "I think she'll help."

Malthooz stirred. "All right," he responded, nodding

slowly. "I can agree with you that there doesn't seem to be any other way. I think it's a big gamble, though."

Lidda grinned.

"But," Malthooz continued, "I'm not going with you."

Lidda tried to object but the half-orc ignored her. He was stalling, trying to work things out in his mind, piecing together the events of the past few hours.

"Look at it this way," he said. "It will be safer for you if you approach the guild alone, and I'll feel better about it. If the situation is the way you think it is, then everything will be fine and it won't matter if I'm with you or waiting somewhere else, but if you're wrong, or even if something happens to you, I'll still be on the loose. I know it's a long shot, but there's always a chance I might come up with a plan on my own."

"I think you're being foolish," she said, "but you're probably right that they wouldn't let me through the back door with you in tow."

The rogue stood up, looking quickly in all directions before stepping out from the jumble of crates where they were hiding.

She paused for a moment and said, "There's an inn close by the guild. It's called the Lock and Keel. We passed it about an hour ago. There's a pair of oars hanging over the door. Do you remember it?"

"I think I can find it."

Lidda smiled and said, "Good. Wait for me there. I don't know how long this will take."

The rogue turned and hustled down the dock. She climbed the ladder two rungs at a time. Seconds later she was gone. Malthooz settled back against a crate. He took a deep breath and looked at the sky. The sun passed behind the white cloth of a sail. By the time it hit the line of hills on the far side of the harbor, he'd have his answer, the half-orc thought.

Moments later, he was on his feet. He wasn't sure what compelled him or what he hoped to find as he climbed the ladder and stepped onto the street. The cleric had called it faith. He was acting on no more than a hunch, he knew, but at least his intuition hadn't recently been proven to be riddled with flaws. It was as good a place to put his trust as any other, Malthooz thought as he set out for the Bung and Blade.

He moved purposefully along the waterfront, believing that he would attract less attention if he looked as if he knew where he was going. At the same time, he kept an eye out for the city watch. Sailors and stevedores passed him by without a glance as he made his way to the nearest alley. Malthooz had no clear idea how cities of this size functioned. It seemed amazing that anyone could keep track of so much activity, let alone keep tabs on everyone or find a particular person. He moved along quiet, narrow, shadowed streets as much as possible, and joined in jostling crowds where necessary. Half-orcs were not that common in Newcoast. He paused a few times to hide amidst the rubbish and barrels crammed into the narrow spaces between buildings.

When at last he rounded the corner of a narrow lane that ran behind the Bung and Blade, the breath caught in his throat and he jumped back into the shadows.

As he'd feared, the inn was being watched. A member of the city guard stood at each end of the alley, and two more stood near the front entrance. That left little hope that he could sneak into the place, though the thought of his pack of books lying in the room upstairs made him long to try. The sleepy, bored look of the guards was almost enough to make him believe he could do it. One of them leaned against the building grooming his fingernails with a short knife while two others tossed a cupful of dice beneath the front window of the common room.

The official presence didn't seem to be frightening off any

customers. Malthooz watched a knot of patrons make their way through the front door. Then again, from what he'd tasted of this city, murder and thievery were everyday occurrences.

"Damn," he cursed softly.

At least he knew for a fact that he and Lidda were still wanted, that even in a city this size, the guard still held hope of finding them. Malthooz turned to go, but stopped. Another figure stood in the shadows near the front of the pub. A dark cowl covered the person's head and hid his face. He appeared to be thin and of average height, dressed in a plain, dark cloak. One of the dice-casting guards stood up and approached the man. Malthooz saw the guard surreptitiously take something from the mysterious figure and stuff it in his pocket. The figure then stepped from the shadow and slipped down the road, disappearing from the half-orcs sight around the nearest corner.

Malthooz shook his head. His imagination would get the best of him if he allowed himself to see conspiracy in every transaction. He turned to go. If even the city guards were corrupt in Newcoast, he thought, then he still had a lot to learn about cities.

"I am as surprised and shocked over the wizard's sudden death as you are," Eva Flint said, offering Lidda a seat. "If the city hadn't come sniffing around the guild for clues I'd have been content to let your friends rot in a cell, convinced that you killed him in order to seize the staff for yourselves. As it is now, I'm told that I am a prime suspect."

She poured herself a glass of wine from the carafe on her desk and offered one to Lidda.

"I can't afford to have anyone breathing down my neck. It's bad for business. I do have certain privileges in this city." She rolled the word privileges luxuriously around her tongue. "Unfortunately, murder isn't one of them. Besides," she said grinning, "I'd hate to see a sister go down."

"That's' not a very reassuring tone," Lidda said. "If we wanted the staff, we never would have come back with it."

The guild master laughed.

"Don't misunderstand me," she said, raising her hand. "It is still in my interest to help you. It's just gotten more compli-cated." She gave Lidda a sly wink. "I need a favor."

Lidda nodded and said, "The gnolls."

Eva refilled her glass.

"No," she said, "although I think the wizard played us both for saps on that score."

"So what do you need me to do?"

"I need you to leave the city," she said.

"That's all?"

"That, and you'll likely not want to show your faces in these parts for quite some time, if ever."

"Because of the murder," Lidda said.

Flint nodded and replied, "I can help you get your friends out of the dungeon, but then I need you to disappear. That will cement your guilt in the eyes of the magistrates. You get your friends back, and I get the city off my back and my name cleared in this business."

She motioned toward the door at the side of her chamber and the doorman entered.

"This is Kargle," she told Lidda. "I believe you've met before. He's going to help you."

Lidda studied the man, for the first time in adequate light. His body was wrapped in a tight-fitting suit of supple leather armor that covered him completely, from his neck to his ankles and from his shoulders to his wrists. Over this, he wore a plain, gray cloak. His eyes were deep brown and set far back in his skull, accenting his hollow cheeks. He looked to be middle aged, though with the physical conditioning of a much younger man. A short sword was strapped to his side, but Lidda was certain that other weapons were hidden in his armor and the folds of his cloak. He bowed to the rogue and offered his hand.

"Will be a pleasure to work with you, m'lady."

Lidda blushed in spite of herself, hearing Kargle refer to her as he did the guild master.

"While I hold the favor of many in positions of power,"

Flint said, moving around her desk, "petty officials can be boringly obtuse when they decide to do things by the book. I've done what I can from a distance, but you're still going to need a little help setting your friends free."

The poor fool, the guild master thought, as Kargle closed the door behind Lidda and himself. That mattered little to her now, though. Even if she had grown to like the halfling's style, the mayor required something to show for the wizard's death.

Yauktul entered the chamber and moved to her side.

"Ah, my pet," she said, rubbing the commander's head. "You've done well this time."

She strode to the wall and picked up the staff from the shelf where it lay. The gnoll followed her every movement with its eyes, its tongue hanging from the side of its mouth. The guild master touched the tip of the artifact to the creature's hands and its eyes rolled back.

"Yes," Flint said, "you have done well, but there is one more thing that you must do."

She pulled the staff away. Yauktul whimpered and yelped as the thing slipped from his touch. He kneeled before Flint and pawed at her boots.

"Get up," the guild master said, kicking at Yauktul's claws.

The guild master walked to her desk and snatched up her wine glass. Things were going to work out fine, she thought. All of her problems would soon be out of her hair. The mayor would have bodies to show the city council, and she would have the staff free and clear.

There was a knock on the wall and four men entered Flint's room through a concealed door behind her desk.

The assassins assembled themselves in front of the guild master. They were lean and wiry like the doorman, but their movements evidenced a suppleness and level of training that few could approach.

Skintight black suits wrapped each of the men, showing the deep ripples of muscle on their chests. They bowed to the guild master as she moved down the line.

None of the men betrayed any emotion in his eyes. Flint grabbed one of them by the chin and gazed into the grim, black orbs. She shuddered minutely. Where even the most hardened of criminals leaked at least a hint of humanity in their gaze, here Flint saw a pit of unfeeling nothingness.

"And you," she said, "are my insurance."

Lidda was taking a long time in returning. Malthooz had been hiding near the inn for almost two hours by the time he finally saw her pass under the torchlight of the street lamp. Kargle rounded the corner behind the halfling. Malthooz didn't like it already. There was something odd about the man, even aside from his unexpected presence with the rogue. Maybe it was just knowing that he was from the guild that made the half-orc suspicious.

He watched them approach. The man's body seemed to melt into the shadows as he moved. His feet made no sound on the cobbles. Malthooz clenched his fists.

"W-who is this?" he stuttered.

He didn't really know what he was expecting from the rogue's trip to the guild. He hadn't worked his way through that part. The situation seemed so hopeless that he hadn't wanted to think about the details. Part of him was hoping that she'd just have the others with her when she came back. He realized how silly that was.

"What a welcome," Lidda said sarcastically. "The wizard is dead. The magic staff is gone. Someone set us up. Give me some credit, Malthooz. Flint offered to help us rescue our friends, and unless you come up with a better plan, I think that you need to trust her."

Malthooz looked at the man.

"And that's what you're for, to help us?" he asked.

"You could say that," the man said, stepping forward. "While the guild has reached a certain level of understanding with the city's officials regarding crime, some things are still considered off limits. For instance," he smiled, "killing innocent wizards. While m'lady Flint is given certain protections from the law, she is not above punishment. My name is Kargle."

Kargle offered Malthooz his hand. The half-orc considered what he was hearing. It wasn't completely implausible. He took Kargle's hand and shook it limply. The man's grip was tremendous.

"What of the others?" Malthooz asked.

"Flint's made arrangements for a jail break," Lidda said, "and for our safe passage from the city. It's not ideal, but we have few other options."

It didn't sound good to the half-orc, but the rogue was right. Leaving the city would be like an admission of guilt, but he had no desire to stay longer in Newcoast anyway. What other choice did he have? He was tired of letting the situation and his own helplessness make his decisions for him.

"Here," said Kargle, handing him a small weapon. "We might not need them, but you never know."

Malthooz looked at the instrument in his hand. It consisted of a stout handle that was affixed to a hard ball of leather. A thin cord, about as long as the span of a hand, separated the two. The cable was flexible, but only slightly so.

"It's a blackjack," Kargle said. "Hit someone on the back of the head and you're almost guaranteed to knock him cold. It's not usually fatal, but you don't want to put all of your strength into it."

Kargle emphasized the last line by striking the small leather weapon against his open hand.

Malthooz palmed the thing and asked, "So what do we do?"

Kargle ran them briefly through the plan. It sounded easy enough to the half-orc, providing that Flint's contacts came through on their end. Something about the way that Kargle spoke still bothered Malthooz, but he was not able to place his finger on it, and at this point he was in a poor position to do anything but follow the man's lead anyway. They started moving.

The night air was cold and crisp as the three made their way through the town. There was not a cloud in the sky, and the stars were visible seemingly by the thousands. Malthooz wished fervently that none of this had ever happened and that he was at home, lying on his back in a field, enjoying the view of the firmament. His friends would be safe and he'd never have laid eyes on the damned staff. He stepped past Lidda and under the light of the street lamp, following Kargle as they started for the jailhouse. Lidda fell in behind him.

The jail was one of a cluster of official buildings near the center of the city. It was an impressive structure. It wasn't nearly as tall as the city hall, but it looked like it was built to withstand a siege. Malthooz read the inscriptions on the marble buildings as they moved past them, wondering exactly what a Temple of Justice was.

"There is no one around," he said, glancing down the wide street.

"Most city business is done during daylight hours," Kargle explained. "And Eva has seen to it that the city guard is not going to bother us."

They came to the broad staircase that ran up to the twin doors at the front of the building.

"Remember," Kargle said over his shoulder as they approached the steps, "only three guards will be on duty inside, and the jailer is not to be harmed."

Malthooz felt a knot forming in the pit of his stomach. It was not just nerves again. If Flint could keep the guards from the streets, she could just as easily have been the one who sent the guards after their group in the first place. His head started swimming as the puzzle that he had constructed in his mind shattered and all of the pieces he'd carefully laid in place flew apart. Suddenly he knew where he had seen the door-man before.

Things were moving much too fast for Malthooz's liking. He felt a desperate need to sit quietly somewhere and think.

Was Lidda in on this, too? Or was she as clueless about the guild's connection to the murder as he had been? He wondered if Kargle had seen the look of recognition cross his face. He cursed the man, wishing that he could get just a moment alone with Lidda. It mattered little if Kargle was aware of what he knew. If they were heading into a trap, the doorman could care less either way. Malthooz had to find a chance to speak with Lidda, to try and discover if she was in on the plot. He had to know whether she had sold them out for a greater share of the gold or a position within the guild. He felt sick. Not more than a few hours ago, he trusted the woman with his life.

"We are going to have to work fast," Kargle said as they neared the door. "By the time we enter the building, the door to the cell should already be open."

He looked at both of them to make sure they were listening before going on.

"The guards are generally in a room just to the right of the entry hall. Farther down that hallway and beyond the main room are the stairs that lead down to the cells."

Kargle rapped the blackjack on his hand.

"If one of the guards escapes and alerts others, we're sunk. I will lead you all to the stables on the south edge of the city when we're done. You will be given mounts and seen past the city wall. At that point you are on your own."

"It'll be just like at the gnoll camp, only easier," Lidda said, elbowing Malthooz in the ribs.

He grabbed her arm as Kargle stepped through the outer doorway.

"Trap," he mouthed to her as he turned to follow the doorman in.

He didn't want to risk turning around to see if the rogue saw his warning. He wasn't sure whether he was more afraid of what lay ahead or the look that he might see on her face.

If **Malthooz had** turned to look, he would have seen the rogue struggling to contain her emotions. Had she understood him correctly? If it had been Krusk, she would have expected the warning as a matter of course. Even though Malthooz shared the barbarian's skepticism, he'd always been one for measured judgement. Certainly he tended to err on the side of timidity as far as danger went, but this was a serious charge. Lidda wasn't eager to lose what remained of her grasp on the guild, but was as that all it was? Could she really have been so foolish? It didn't matter now if it was. Her chances of working for the thieves guild again were getting slimmer by the minute, at least in Newcoast.

She tried to reason her way through it. What interest would Flint have in getting them out of the way? Wotherwill's murder could be blamed on them whether they were alive or dead, present or absent. So why have them killed?

If Kargle read the concern on her face, he didn't show it.

"The guards will be in a room to the right not far past this door," he said, looking back at Malthooz as they approached a second set of doors. "The rogue and I will knock them out and you can cover the door to make sure no one else comes in or leaves."

He reached into a pocket in the chest of his armor and pulled out a lock pick. Even in her agitated state, Lidda had to marvel at the man's skill. With years of practice and experience, she still did not posses the easy flair with which Kargle undid the lock. He inserted the tool and with a quick flick of his wrist, the mechanism snapped open.

For that matter, Lidda thought, watching Kargle drop the pick into his armor and reach for the handle, why didn't Flint just go right for the staff herself? And where did the gnolls fit into it all?

Kargle moved down the short hallway. He stopped outside the door of the guardroom. Lidda crept up to his side, fingering the blackjack. She glanced back at Malthooz standing near the door and saw the worry in his eyes. If he was right, then getting Kargle out of the way now might be the best thing she could do.

It certainly wasn't beyond the guild master to double-cross anyone. If the price was right, it was probably Flint's preferred method. She could profit triple-fold. There would be the wizard's money when he paid for the artifact's passage, more of it when she brokered the wizard's hiring of the adventurers, and the final payoff of keeping the staff for herself.

Lidda felt Kargle's eyes on her. A grin slid across his lips as he tapped the end of the blackjack against the side of his leg and started toward the guardroom.

If the Deepwood didn't do them in, Flint's gnoll should have, but that was where Flint made her error. She didn't count on the group's success. Lidda shrugged. It was now or never, as she saw it.

She swung the blackjack hard across the back of Kargle's head. The knot on the top of the weapon struck the man's skull with a thud, and his body crumpled to the floor. She looked at him for a few moments, then back at the startled Malthooz.

"So much for the help," she quipped. "Let's go get our friends."

Krusk was bored. He'd paced the cell all afternoon, stopping occasionally only to shake the bars and curse at the guards upstairs. The women took the barbarian's impatience in stride. They'd long since realized the futility of trying to calm him down and figured that he'd tire sooner or later.

They just didn't know how much later.

"That damned rogue better do something soon," he fumed. "If she leaves town, I'll—"

"Whoa, Krusk," Vadania said, jumping up and moving to the barbarian's side. "You know she'd never even think of leaving us here."

She steered him over to Mialee and forced him to sit down.

The wizard patted his shoulder and said, "Easy, boy."

Krusk was ablaze with anger. Most of the day had been spent composing a mental list of all the people he intended to throttle when he got out of the dungeon. Eva Flint was at the top, but Lidda was right behind in second place.

Krusk knew what friendship was. He certainly knew what loyalty was. What he didn't appreciate was patience.

"I don't care if Flint had nothing to do with any of it," he growled. "I want to kick her head into a basket."

The spot of light that shone through the cell's shaft to the outside world crawled across the floor and halfway up the opposite wall as the day wore on. As evening fell, the frustration of imprisonment was wearing at them all.

It was a welcome respite from boredom when a guard

made his way to their cell with the evening meal. Tin platters clattered across stones as the man set them on the ground and slid them through a gap in the bars.

"It's not much," he said, "but probably more than you deserve."

Krusk no longer had the energy to curse the man. His anger was focused elsewhere.

Vadania collected the plates and gave one to each of her companions before grabbing her own and taking a seat on the straw next to Mialee. A thin stew sloshed across the bottom of the plates. Krusk pushed the liquid around with a hard chunk of stale bread before managing a bite. It was awful. He'd have thrown it back at the guard if not for his gnawing hunger.

The jailer returned a while later with two guards in tow. They moved slowly down the row of cells, collecting plates and replacing chamber pots. The guards stood outside the cells with crossbows drawn as the jailer went in after the used urns.

"Don't try it," Vadania said, squeezing Krusk's arm as the jailer opened the door to their cell.

The guard kept a wary eye and a crossbow pointed at the barbarian as the jailer dropped an urn in the rear of their cell and grabbed the old one. Krusk growled as the man passed him by and exited the cell. The jailer shut the door and turned the key with an odd grin before moving on to the next cell.

Krusk saw Mialee's ears perk and watched her and Vadania exchange looks. The druid held her hand up to her mouth. A few minutes later, they heard the heavy door at the top of the staircase slam shut.

Mialee jumped up and moved to the door of the cell. She looked up and down the hallway, then gave the door a kick. It swung open. The barbarian was on his feet at once.

"It's our chance," he said through clenched teeth, "and we'll take it now."

"Is it broken?" Vadania asked. "Did he use the wrong key?"

"I don't know, and I don't care," Mialee said. "Maybe it's pure luck. I'm not asking questions or waiting for answers."

"Nor I," said Krusk. "I can handle those guards if I have a little room to maneuver."

"What if there are others?" the druid asked.

"So much the worse for them," Krusk replied. "You can stay and worry about their welfare if you want to, but I'm getting out of here.

"Coming?" he asked.

Krusk glared menacingly at the other prisoners as he passed down the row of cells.

"Make so much as a peep and I'll snap all of your necks," he growled.

Lidda hugged the wall as she moved around the door frame. She crouched low to the ground, circling the table to get herself directly behind the closest of the men seated at the large, round table that filled the room. A rack of weapons hung from the wall opposite the rogue. She found herself wishing that she'd taken more time to study the place before going in. Moving silently and unobserved, she crept along the shadows.

"I'm just glad he's down there and we're up—"

The man's words dropped away when Lidda struck the base of his skull with her blackjack. His face landed in stacks of silver and copper pieces, scattering them. The other two men jumped back as the nimble halfling sprang from behind the fallen man's chair and launched herself directly across the table. She grabbed the nearest guard by the collar of his leather armor and smashed the blackjack across his face. His head snapped to the side with the impact of the blow, spittle and pieces of his teeth flying from his bloody mouth.

The last one lunged for a short sword that hung on the wall

just beyond his reach. His hand closed short of the hilt of the weapon as Lidda's arms closed around his neck. The man spun around to place the rogue between himself and the wall and threw his body backward, crushing the rogue with his weight. The blow pushed the wind from Lidda's lungs. Her arms loosened slightly as she struggled to get a breath. Black spots danced in her vision. She groped for the man's eyes as she felt her ribcage being crushed.

"Malthooz, you fool," she managed to gasp as the guard reached around and grabbed a handful of her hair.

Where is that idiot?

Malthooz ran through the door. He came around the table with his blackjack raised. Desperately, the guard slammed Lidda against the wall again, and she fell to the floor gasping for breath. The man grabbed a weapon from the rack and moved to intercept Malthooz.

"I won't hold it against you if you give up now," the guard said, laughing. "I'm sure we have room for you and your friend downstairs."

He swung the sword. Malthooz leaped back, narrowly avoiding the blade.

"Then again," the guard said, "I could just kill you now and keep the paperwork to a minimum."

Lidda rolled herself over, the handle of the blackjack in her hand. The guard caught her movement in the corner of his eye and spun around. His boot shot out, catching the rogue in the side, but his foot was too slow. The leather weapon flew from Lidda's outstretched arm. It sailed at the man's face, end over end, to strike him in the forehead.

Malthooz jumped forward as the man reacted to the clout. The half-orc grabbed the guard's neck, intending to steady him for a knockout blow. A jolt of energy flowed from his hand and traveled into the man's body. Malthooz yanked his hand away. The man convulsed once and went down.

Lidda got up slowly from the floor, clutching her side, and said, "I may have broken a rib or two."

"Let me," Malthooz said moving to her side.

"Save it. I'm not sure your newfound powers would be enough to deal with this anyway."

They heard the clatter of footsteps coming up the stairs. Lidda grabbed two swords from the rack on the wall and tossed one of the unfamiliar weapons to the half-orc.

"Just swing it like a club," she advised. "We can't be choosy right now. Sounds like a crowd coming up the steps. How much more of that magic do you have in you?"

Malthooz shrugged.

"It just seems to happen," he whispered. "I can't really control it."

"Well, keep it happening," Lidda said.

Malthooz smiled. It was good to have his companion back and to shelve his doubts about her loyalty. Even if they didn't make it out of this place alive, at least he wouldn't die alone. Lidda raised her sword and moved behind the table as the footsteps sounded just outside the door.

Malthooz tensed as the door burst open. He saw Krusk's large form charge through the open portal, followed quickly by Mialee. A moment later, Vadania entered the room. She stopped short and looked over the unexpected scene.

"I thought this escape was too easy to be true," she said.

Krusk seemed to be struggling with whether he should hug Malthooz or strangle Lidda. Instead, he stood dumbfounded, unable to speak.

"We're happy to see you too, Krusk," Lidda said, letting her sword arm fall. She nodded at the unconscious guards lying about the room. "I thought I'd have to put a few more to rest when I heard you coming up the stairs."

"Is this Flint's doing?" Mialee asked.

Lidda nodded. "Yeah, but I think we have more trouble on the way."

"The body in the hallway?" Vadania asked.

"His name is Kargle," Lidda replied. "Doorman from the guild. Apparently he was Flint's right hand man. I wasn't sure if he was a help or a hindrance, but when Malthooz decided we were walking into a trap, I figured it was best to get him out of the way for safety's sake. It just seemed prudent."

"I knew it," Krusk said.

"Yeah," Lidda said with a sigh, "and I should have guessed it. I let myself get too caught up in the idea of joining the guild to see clearly."

"So where's the ambush?" Krusk asked. "Don't try to tell me that Flint expected these three to keep us here."

"No, I think that's what Kargle was for," Lidda said, "but let's not wait around to find out."

"Are you all right to move, Lidda?" Mialee asked.

"I can move," she replied, though the pain in her side grew more acute with each passing minute.

Krusk took a sword from the rack on the wall. He grabbed the hair of the guard who was slumped over the table and pressed the blade against the unconscious man's neck. Lidda grabbed his arm.

"Don't do it Krusk. They're just doing their jobs."

"Was part of that job to harass and insult me?" The barbarian glared momentarily, but withdrew the blade and satisfied himself with slamming the man's face down onto the table. A few coins clattered to the floor. Krusk hit the back of the guard's skull with the pommel of his sword and added, "That's for the gag."

When everyone was armed, they started toward the front doors. At the sound of someone moving behind them, Krusk spun around and saw a door slam shut at the far end of the hallway. The barbarian bolted in pursuit, breaking the door down as he went. The old jailer was huddled in the corner at the far end of the chamber. His whole frame shivered in fear as the barbarian approached him.

"Anything you want," the man pleaded, throwing up his hands.

The others filed in. The place was filled with row upon row of cabinets, each of them clasped and locked.

"Looks like we found our stuff," Lidda said, tossing aside the cheap blade she held.

Krusk grabbed the ring of keys the jailer held out to him.

Cold air greeted them when they emerged from the jailhouse. The marble stairs in front of the building ran down into a broad avenue. Oil-fed lights flickered up and down the lane, casting a pale glow on the cobbled stones that paved the avenue. Though they gave better illumination than the primitive torches that lined the streets in the shabbier quarters, they left much to be desired.

Krusk wiped Kargle's blood from the blade of his dagger and returned it to the sheath on his forearm. He looked at the tall, stone architecture around him as he stood on the top step. The area was far different from the places he was used to, with wooden construction and the bustle of people at all hours. He scanned the windows for signs of life but light glowed in few of them. The barbarian knew enough of cities to know that this part of town was largely abandoned after sundown, its officers and officials having long since conducted their business and gone home to mansions on the hills above the bay. He also knew that the area was likely to be patrolled by at least a modest number of guards.

"Looks like everyone's gone home," Mialee said, joining Krusk at the front of the landing. "I wonder if the guild's influence is enough to keep the eyes of the watch occupied."

"According to the man that Krusk just gutted, it is," Lidda said.

Krusk growled.

"Don't worry, Krusk," the rogue added. "Kargle was no friend of mine. He deserved it."

The barbarian started down the steps and into the street, headed straight for the heart of the market district.

"Where are you going?" Lidda asked, stopping the barbarian short. The quickest way out of the city is over here," she said, pointing in the opposite direction. "We have our chance, let's take it."

But Krusk had been pushed farther than he was willing to be pushed. He knew that the rogue's words made sense, but he refused to let himself see it. The guild had played him for a patsy, and he was going to have revenge. Anyone who got in his way would get bowled over.

"Flint's going to pay with her life before the night is up," he said through clenched teeth.

"Fool," the rogue replied. "You can't get into that guild unless they let you."

Krusk patted the blade of his axe and said, "I have my invitation right here."

"You're both fools," Vadania hissed. She moved down the stairs, her eyes scanning the rooftops nearby. "There's a half dozen places from which we could be fired on and numerous alleyways from which ambush might come. Do you really think Flint would let us go so easily?"

"I'm hoping she wouldn't," Krusk replied.

As Krusk turned away, a crossbow bolt flew past Mialee's head and smashed into the stone doorframe of the jailhouse. Others whistled by and clattered all around the companions.

Krusk looked up to see the dark form of a sniper pop up from behind a rooftop parapet and fire on him.

"The rooftops," Krusk hollered, leaping back up the steps for the cover of the doorway.

"Just like I said," Vadania replied. "Are you ever going to learn to listen, Krusk?"

The barbarian growled at the druid, "If you had listened to me from the beginning, we wouldn't be anywhere near here now."

He grabbed the dagger from his forearm, ducked around the corner, and hurled it at the first moving shape he saw. The blade sailed through the darkness to catch the assailant in the throat. A crossbow rattled to the ground, the body of a gnoll right behind it.

"More gnolls!" Krusk snarled. "We finish this now!"

He sprinted out into the street, moving from doorway to doorway down the avenue with the others huddled in a tight knot behind him. Missiles bounced off the stones around them as they moved. Krusk hustled into an alcove and threw his shoulder into a door. The wood splintered as his body impacted the surface, but the frame held. The others squeezed in behind the barbarian.

Lidda jiggled the door handle.

"Locked," she said. "I could pick it but I'm not sure I want to be trapped inside."

Eva Flint cursed under her breath at the incompetence of the gnoll snipers. She looked over at their commander with scorn. Yauktul was squatting behind the parapet with his pack, barking orders through his teeth as they reloaded their weapons. The commander's failure at the camp should have been enough to let the guild master know better than to trust the wretch, but she'd let his success with Wotherwill speak too loudly of him.

Everything about the whole affair would have been easier if things had gone according to plan, if the adventurers had been killed at the outpost or if the city had not come snooping around after Wotherwill was removed from the list of players. Things hadn't gone according to her design, and they continued to go afoul.

"Where the hell is Kargle?" she spat, slamming a gloved fist into the stone battlement. "He was supposed to kill them all inside the jail house."

Between her assassin and the guards, the adventurers should have been easy prey. At least some of them should have died in jail, leaving only a few for the gnolls to finish off. It seemed, however, that nothing but error and folly had befallen her from the start. She was beginning to wonder if the tales of the staff really were true. It certainly seemed to have rattled Yauktul. He'd been useless since his return. He whimpered something about losing his finest troops to the enemy and, judging by the aim of those sniping from the roof, she was inclined to believe him.

All she wanted was the staff's value in gold. Its magic could be damned, as far as she cared. She made a mental note never to work with a wizard again.

Unwilling to peer over the parapet herself lest one of the victims recognized her, she looked over at the gnolls. Yauktul's tongue hung from the side of his snout. He even looked incompetent, Flint thought, nothing like the killer she'd sent out. At least he agreed with her on something. They had to be prepared for the unexpected once the jailbreak began, beyond just the crossbows. If he was useless in every other respect, at least the gnoll was good at agreeing.

"Hold your fire," Flint said, motioning across her neck with a hand. "Let's move into the street. You're accomplishing nothing from here."

The gnolls filed down a ladder into the building. Flint got to her knees and chanced a quick glance over the wall before joining them. She smiled as her foot hit the first rung and she disappeared into the hatch.

Flint had seen the four dark shapes moving down the street toward her targets.

"I've been hit," Malthooz announced in disbelief.

He groaned, feeling for the first time the full pain in his back just under his shoulder blade. The back of his tunic was stained red, a crimson patch growing slowly down his side as the blood leaked from the wound. The feathered end of a crossbow bolt stuck from his skin. The bolt was buried deep in his body, if the small tip still visible was an indication. His arm tingled and he felt himself losing sensation in his fingertips.

Malthooz had felt the impact when the bolt hit, like being punched in the shoulder, but he'd thought someone had bumped into him. It was only when he slammed his back against the hard wall and felt the shaft grind inside his shoulder that he realized the truth.

Krusk knelt down next to him and examined the wound. Malthooz howled as the barbarian probed with his finger inside the wound, feeling for the head of the missile.

"It's gone in deep, too deep to get it out here," he said.

The swarthy color was draining from Malthooz's face, and he slumped against the closed door. Krusk supported him as he slid down the wood, leaving a dark streak of blood down the rough surface.

"No, it's best to leave it," Lidda said, with an edge of fear in her voice. "It'll slow the bleeding."

"We have to find shelter quickly or we'll all be sprouting little sticks with feathers," Mialee said coldly, eyeing the street. "Maybe we can find an open building down by the wharves."

"With who knows how many gnolls firing on us the whole way?" Vadania asked, slamming the wall with her fist in frustration. "We'd be cut to shreds."

"What other choice do we have?" Lidda yelled at the druid.

"Hsst." Krusk ran a hand across his throat, pointing with the other at the black-clad figures approaching from across the street. "We're out of time. There're no choices left to make."

He let Malthooz down to the ground and propped him sitting up in the doorway. Malthooz sighed as his body came to rest on the cool stones. His eyes lost their focus and the fear on his face was replaced with a peaceful calm.

"Go," he said, "leave me here. You can't help me and I can't help you."

His head sank back against the wall and his hand slipped into the front of his shirt, where the wooden symbol of Pelor hung.

The men in the street were drawing closer, closing in across the square toward the companions. Krusk could make out four of them. Their every movement was graceful. Too skilled, Krusk thought, to be part of the city watch.

"The crossbows have stopped," Lidda said, peeking around the corner. "Too bad. Maybe they would have hit one of those killers by mistake." She moved into the street, drawing her sword.

Krusk rested his hand against Malthooz's brow. The half-orc stirred at the touch of skin. His eyes opened and he lifted his head from the wall. His lips moved as though he was about to speak, but he had nothing to say. He just smiled at Krusk and let his head fall back against the wall.

"I'll stay with him," Vadania said. She put her hand on Krusk's shoulder. "I'll do what I can. Lidda and Mialee need your help."

A grim determination settled over Krusk. His concern for Malthooz slipped away as he felt the reassurance of anger overtaking his mind. The rage that had simmered all afternoon boiled to the surface. He had been tricked, cheated, and imprisoned. His friend, a half-orc like himself, was dying before Krusk's eyes. Someone was going to pay. He raised the axe above his head and erupted into the street.

The four assassins fanned themselves out in the open street as Krusk flew past Lidda and bore down on them like a charging bull.

Each of the men wielded a different weapon. The tallest of them brandished a katana and a small, spiked shield. Behind him came another swinging a long, spiked chain that he held by two circular handles that were equally spaced from the fist-sized, spiked balls at either end of the chain. The spikes on the chain were matched by those the man wore strapped on his hands. The last two moved almost as though they were one. They were identical by all appearance, the similarity following through even to the long, curved daggers they held in each of their hands. The assassins stepped up to meet Krusk's charge as the barbarian thundered across the space between them.

Krusk's axe met the assassin's katana in a ringing of steel and a shower of sparks. Instantly the man crouched down, deflecting Krusk's weapon to the side then swinging his blade back at the barbarian as he rolled away. It was a defensive strike with little power, and Krusk simply let the blow land. He wasn't interested in defending himself, only in attacking. The katana struck his armor, sliced through the leather, and bit a shallow gash across the half-orc's ribs. Without pausing or flinching, Krusk spun to face the circling assassin.

The barbarian's heavy axe was no match for the swiftness of the man's sword, nor was Krusk half as agile. The barbarian moved in on the swordsman with his full bulk, ignoring the katana while he set up a smashing blow. The assassin held his weapon ready, backing away as the barbarian came on.

Krusk rushed in with his axe held high over his head. He knew he was leaving himself wide open to the man's attack, but he also knew that the pinprick of the sword would never stop him before his axe split the man's skull. The assassin thrust his blade as he dodged to the side, away from the sweeping axe. Krusk felt the weapon slice his thigh as he rushed past.

The cut felt like no more than a sting through Krusk's rage. He spun again and rushed back, much faster than the assassin expected. Again the man tried to dodge and slash, but Krusk had just seen that maneuver. With a slight twist, he let the katana bite into the heavy leather protecting his gut. The keen edge sliced into the armor just deep enough to draw blood, and there it lodged. Realization froze the assassin for only a split-second, but that was all Krusk wanted. His axe whistled downward, cleaving through the swordsman's right shoulder, ribs, and spine, stopping only when it struck the pelvis. The body peeled away in a butchered mess on the pavement. A quick snatch freed the shivering katana from Krusk's armor. With a sneer, the barbarian set the tip against the pavement and stomped on the blade, shattering it into slivers.

The twins circled to either side of Lidda in an obvious attempt to flank the rogue. Obvious, but effective, she thought. She would have to choose one to attack, and when she did, the other would stab her in the back. No subtlety needed. Lidda backed up, biting her lip, trying to buy some time. She couldn't allow one of them to get behind her.

She spun suddenly toward the assassin moving to her right. She took three quick steps forward, waving her sword arm in an obvious threat while her left hand slipped a throwing dagger from the sheath on her thigh. Instead of giving ground as she hoped, the man grinned and stepped ahead to meet her challenge, his twin daggers crossed in front of his chest defensively.

"I should have guessed that you wouldn't opt for even odds," Lidda said to the approaching twin. Before he could respond in any way, she spun and threw the dagger into the throat of his partner, who had advanced silently to within only feet of her unprotected back. Without a pause, she was again facing the first antagonist. "You should know that I have tricks of my own."

Behind her, the man gurgled and clutched at the knife hilt protruding from his throat. He would have screamed, but the blade was blocking his windpipe. Desperately, he wrenched the weapon from the wound. Blood gushed over the front of his black armor and flooded down the severed windpipe into his lungs. He stumbled backward, letting the knife clatter to the pavement. After two more steps, he fell to the street. His whole frame convulsed with the effort of fighting to get air into his drowning lungs. Lidda heard the commotion and knew that it would continue for a few minutes before the assassin finally blacked out, but he was no threat in that condition.

She grinned and asked, "What do you think of the odds now?"

The man spat, "Only that he was the lesser of us, so the odds haven't changed as much as you think."

At close range, Lidda could see that the two men definitely were twins. The man's coldness over his brother's death chilled her and brought Malthooz back to her mind. She understood that she faced a cruel and calculating killer. The man approached slowly, not rushing to within reach of Lidda's sword. He held one dagger close and near his chest as though it was a shield while he threatened Lidda's defenses with the other. Even armed only with daggers, his arms were long enough to equal Lidda's reach with her sword. With a rapid slash, he swept both knives at the halfling. He was quick as a snake, and Lidda hadn't expected him to use the left-hand dagger so deftly. She dodged one blade by lunging sideways and caught the other with the hilt of her sword. A savage twist sent the stiletto spinning harmlessly away, and she threw her boot up and into the man's ribcage.

She felt more than heard the ribs crack and winced as a streak of pain went up her own side, a reminder from her tangle at the jail. Shrugging off the pain, she tumbled to the side of the man as he spun around. Somehow he had two daggers again, and he slashed with both of them a second time. At the last moment he flipped the weapon in his left hand. The butt of the knife hit the halfling across the jaw. Lidda turned her head with the strike to lessen the effect of the blow but felt the heat of pain spread across her cheek where the pommel of the dagger connected.

She spun around in a complete circle from the force of the dagger, and she used that to feign as if she was going to go down. She fell to her knees, hoping to draw the man closer. He took the bait. As he moved in for the kill, Lidda snapped her sword around in an arc that plunged it into his side.

The assassin doubled over with the blade half buried in his body. Lidda jumpd to her feet, placed both hands on the hilt, and shoved with all her might. The sword pierced completely through his body. The assassin gasped one final time, then toppled sideways. The tip of Lidda's blade struck sparks when it hit the cobblestones.

Mialee wasn't thrilled to be heading into battle without the power of her magic. She'd had no time to prepare herself in the confusion of their arrest and escape. She didn't even know where her spellbook was anymore. At least she had recovered her most essential components, she thought, fingering the pouch hanging at her belt.

She had little time to weigh options, however. A whistling noise alerted her to danger on her left side, and she ducked just as the spiked chain lashed over her head. There was no chance to regain her balance because the weapon whirled continuously, whipping to the left and right without pause. Mialee tried to scramble away but the assassin turned the chain's axis, twirling one of the balls high at the wizard's head and the other low at her legs. The lower one struck first, slicing open her knee and knocking her feet from under her. It also saved her life, because the tumble dropped her head below the whistling arc of the second spiked ball. She rolled away desperately, trying to get beyond the chains' reach.

The wizard pulled herself up to her knees then to her feet as the assassin circled. She shifted her weight from one leg to the other experimentally, and breathed a sigh of relief that her kneecap wasn't shattered. She dodged the chain again, but winced as her weight came down on the injured leg. Blood from the wound trickled into her boot.

The assassin smiled at her, twirling the chain slowly in a double figure-eight pattern.

"I swear, if I had my magic . . ." Mialee cursed.

A flick of the assassin's wrist sent one of the balls straight at Mialee's head. She threw her sword up and deflected the deadly missile, but was too slow to move away from the second one that was again sweeping in at her legs. The cold steel of the chain struck against her leg and the weight of the weapon wrapped around it. Before Mialee fully realized what happened, she felt the spikes slice into her calf. The assassin yanked, pulling both handles up over his head, and Mialee tumbled to the stones in a heap.

He fell upon her at once. His spiked fist slammed the cobblestones beside the wizard's head, but she jerked from side to side rapidly to avoid the blows. She couldn't avoid his other fist, however, when it slammed down hard on her stomach. Air rushed from her lungs to be replaced by stabbing pain.

"If you had your magic, you'd what?" he sneered, raising his arm and placing one of the spikes under her chin.

Mialee gasped for breath. Spots of light flickered in her vision and tears flooded her eyes. She felt the tip of the steel spike on her flesh.

Her free hand groped into the pouch at her belt. She grabbed the first thing that her fingers fell upon and frantically tossed a handful of it into the man's face. Yellow granules of sulfur flew into his eyes and nostrils. He reeled back, coughing and wheezing. The hand around Mialee's neck loosened and the spike fell away. She kicked up, catching the assassin between his legs. He groaned and rolled to the side. The wizard pushed herself out from underneath him and scrambled crablike across the street, still gagging and struggling to refill her lungs with breath.

She nearly screamed when a huge shape burst into her vision, but instead of attacking her, it planted a massive boot heavily on the assassin's stomach. The man howled in pain, and Mialee heard a loud crack that must have been a rib. She looked at the dark shape standing over them and realized that it was Krusk. His armor, arms, hands, and even his face were drenched in blood. It dripped from the buckles of his breastplate and hung in thickening strands from his axe. It couldn't possibly all be his, Mialee realized, or he couldn't stand. He didn't even glance at her before placing the gory axe blade against the struggling assassin's neck and drawing it slowly across until metal scraped the pavement.

Lidda was at Mialee's side in seconds, tugging her to her feet. "We've got to get back to Malthooz," she urged.

The wizard looked at the purple and black bruise on the rogue's cheek. Mialee let the rogue lift her from the ground. At least she was in good company, she thought, as the three of them limped down the street. Krusk had one hand on the halfling's shoulder and his other draped over the elf's neck. Mialee chuckled softly. She wasn't sure who was helping whom.

They found Malthooz and the druid waiting quietly in the doorway. Mialee was relieved to see that they had not been attacked or disturbed by any other assailants. Her relief faded as she stepped into the doorway, and disappeared entirely when she saw the grim look on Vadania's face.

"It is not good," the druid said as the three approached.

Malthooz lay against the door. His eyes were closed. A ragged bandage torn from the druid's cloak was wrapped around his chest. The bolt, still shiny with the half-orc's blood, lay on the cobblestones a few feet away. Mialee saw the shallow rise and fall of Malthooz's ribs. At least he's still alive, she thought. He stirred as they drew close.

"I've done all I can for him," Vadania said. "Without more magic, I can offer him little. My herbs can only do so much."

Malthooz smiled at the sight of his friends. His mouth moved, but his breath was too shallow to actually speak. He reached for the symbol of Pelor on his chest and raised it shakily. He wanted to remove it, but his head was against the wall. Krusk took his hand and cradled Malthooz's head away from the wall with his other arm, then he lifted the cord that held the holy symbol over his friend's head and handed it to him. Malthooz smiled.

"Thank you," he mouthed, nodding at Krusk's open hand.

Malthooz fingered the disk for a moment, then offered the symbol to Krusk.

"Take it," Vadania said when Krusk hesitated.

The barbarian took the thing from Malthooz's hand and placed it around his own neck. Malthooz smiled broadly.

Eva Flint rounded the corner of the building and stepped into the street. She fell back immediately into the shadow, startled at the sight that befell her. Her assassins lay in broken heaps on the slush-covered cobblestones, their weapons scattered amidst the red snow. The adventurers were again huddled in the doorway where the gnolls had penned them with their crossbows.

She cursed them, thinking about how deep a hole she'd dug herself into. Her judgment of her foes could not have been more wrong. She spat. There were four more bodies to explain, on top of Wotherwill's and likely a handful of jailhouse guards. The guild master wasn't sure that the favors she was owed would cover a scandal so big. The mayor might even decide that she was becoming an embarrassment, too much of a liability, and try to shut down the guild for a few months. That would be a disaster.

The guild master watched her enemies moving off, the barbarian holding the limp body of the other half-orc in his arms. They were walking away from her, toward the far side of the jailhouse. She sneered contemptuously, thinking of all of the planning and effort that managed to kill only one of the five, and it was the feeble one at that.

She grabbed Yauktul by the throat.

"This is the ultimate test," she said. Still gripping the terrified gnoll, she drew the staff from her belt and pressed it into the creature's shaking paws. "Take this damned thing, and don't fail me now."

The gnoll clutched the device to his chest, whimpering and cooing to it as he rubbed the globe on the top of the shaft. The yellow slits of his eyes glassed over and he mouthed silent words to himself.

Flint cursed Wotherwill's name. The artifact had brought her nothing but pain and humiliation, and she was ready to be done with it. It was no longer worth the trouble it caused. Besides, the guild master thought, she had other resources to fall back upon. The staff was worth a lot, surely, but not enough. If she was going to make a clean break from Newcoast, she didn't want the cursed staff spoiling everything all over again.

She patted Yauktul's head. "Get them, my pet. They are the ones who took your treasure, and they will take it again unless you stop them."

The gnoll growled and bared his fangs at Flint's words. His arms hugged the staff more tightly to his chest. Flint stepped back from the pair. She could feel the raw lust to kill radiating from the creature's eyes, now that they were no longer clouded with indecision.

Flint pointed Yauktul out into the street. His row of troops padded chaotically behind their commander, all of them showing the effect of the staff's proximity with their snarling and snapping at one another as each tried move as close as possible to the magical staff. The guild master studied the group coldly. She shook her head. They looked nothing like the savage but disciplined pack she'd dealt with in the past. The staff's presence had twisted them into a mob of slavering incompetents. She had little faith that they would be able to stop the adventurers from escaping.

Flint spun around and bolted for the alleyway. She knew she'd never be able to clear up the mess with the city. It was time for her to leave town. She would be glad to be rid of them all, gnolls and heroes alike. It would be hours before the extent of the night's activities were revealed. Plenty of time to wrap up loose ends and get far away.

Waves of hatred flowed through Yauktul's veins. He watched the companions moving down the road through squinting eyelids as he muttered to himself. Another sound cut through his own soft voice, a buzz of whispered words that echoed through the creature's clouded mind.

Must kill.

He shook his head and looked at his men, but none of them seemed to have heard the voices in his head. The commander waved the artifact to his men, urging them forward. The troopers shuffled along the paved street, following behind the fleeing company.

Yauktul had seen what the group was capable of, how they'd wiped out his elite guard at the camp in the Deepwood as he himself fled into the forest, how they killed the ettin and cut through the rest of his company as though they were nothing. Yes, Yauktul had seen what the group was capable of. He was not eager to face them again.

He commanded his men to stop as another thought hit him between the eyes, causing his legs to twitch and setting his teeth to grinding. The words came more strongly this time, pushing all other thoughts aside.

Must Flee.

Yauktul wanted to get away from the whole affair. The voice urged him to return to the forest, return to the simpler days before he met the guild master and fell into her web of power. He could live in peace in the forest with his new treasure, and keep it safe. Flint promised him wealth and power beyond his wildest dreams, but until the staff was in his hands, he'd seen little to compensate for his hardships and loss. If he left now, everything would be better.

Yauktul remembered what it felt like to be so near the object as he'd carried it from the shipwreck to his camp. The sense of power and wellness that he experienced as it sat in the chest in his tent, the calm it brought him and the lust for murder that its loss invoked. The guild master's face flashed through his mind and the words came back.

Must obey.

Images of the woman filled his brain with a longing for blood. He whimpered softly as he thought of crushing Flint's head with the staff. He could almost feel the side of the thing hitting the woman's skull. He would take the thieves guild for himself, he thought. He'd seen the power and influence that Flint commanded. Yauktul licked his lips. He could control it all. The words raced through his head, tumbling in on top of the others until they were just a steady hum of conflicting directives.

The creature clutched Wotherwill's staff tighter to himself. He paused. Then came the strongest urge.

Must flee.

The words pounded through him, swirling with a force that almost drove him to his knees. Yauktul turned aside for a moment, looking at the brightening sky as he thought of the freedom of the wild. He turned back to face his pack. His troops stared at their commander, waiting for him to give a command, any command. They needed him to lead them, the staff told him, they needed him to give them purpose. They needed him to tell them to kill. Yauktul pawed at the staff.

Must obey.

His foes were slipping away from him. They were the foul things that took his treasure away. They'd made him suffer, and Yauktul would make them pay.

He barked a command to his gnolls and followed after them as they moved down the road.

Yes, the staff told him, *it is time for revenge.*

Krusk grabbed Malthooz under his arm and lifted him from the ground. Malthooz groaned as he was raised to his feet, and his head rolled from side to side as he struggled to look around.

"We've got to go," Krusk said to the others as he turned out of the tiny alcove and moved into the street.

The slash in the barbarian's leg was beginning to throb and burn as the fury of the battle ebbed. The cut in his abdomen hurt, too, but he suspected it was very shallow. The weight of Malthooz brought fresh awareness of both injuries to Krusk even as his fear for the half-orc he carried drove him to move faster. Krusk's breath was short and he felt weary in his bones, but he pushed himself to move, fought through the fatigue as he would battle a physical enemy. Anger at the guild master still burned in the pit of his stomach. Krusk pushed it aside, feeling another, even stronger calling. He had to save Malthooz. The half-orc didn't stand a chance if he didn't get help soon. Krusk also knew that all of them had to get out of Newcoast as quickly as possible. When dawn broke, all hell would break loose, and they would be sitting ducks for the city guard. They had no safe refuge in the city, especially since the guild had turned against them. They had to get out of the city.

"We can head for the forest," Vadania said as she trotted alongside the barbarian. "I might be able to save him, if he makes it to the forest."

Krusk nodded, but he wasn't really listening to the druid. He heard the snow crunch under his boots as he concentrated on every step, counting off each one as another step toward freedom and away from the guild.

As he rounded the corner of the jailhouse, Krusk heard Lidda curse.

"Gnolls," the rogue hissed as she came around the side of the building. "A bunch of them."

Krusk turned at the sound of her voice. She stepped back and paused, as though she was considering whether to say more. Krusk glared at her; he had no more patience for anything. He turned again and resumed his march. There was no time to spare for a fight with the creatures.

Let them come, Krusk thought. I'll deal with them if and when they catch me.

When Lidda spoke again, her words hit Krusk like a fist to the stomach: "Flint's with them."

The tiny thread of restraint snapped in the barbarian's head. Overpowering anger welled up. His limbs, aching from the exertion of the fight, suddenly felt warmer and lighter, renewed by an inner reserve of strength.

"She bolted down an alley," Lidda continued. The rogue pressed her back against the cool marble and peered around the edge. "The dogs are coming this way, but they look confused." An uncharacteristic growl escaped her lips. "The one from the camp is with them."

Malthooz groaned and tried to raise his head.

"Get, her," he said weakly. "None of us is safe while she lives." The half-orc smiled unevenly. "Get her for me."

Vadania went to Krusk's side, but the barbarian brushed her away. He looked at the druid but didn't really recognize her. Next to the wall, Krusk set Malthooz down in the clean snow. When he stood, his axe was in his hands.

The others waited, unsure what would happen next. Krusk backed away from them, shaking his head. The assassin's blood that covered him was shiny and black. His eyes were mere slits, but they glowed with anger. Without a word, the barbarian turned on his heel and jogged back the way they had come.

"I'm going with him," Lidda announced. "Not even Krusk can chop his way into the guild hall. He's going to need help."

Mialee said, "Nothing but death will stop him now. Go with him, and watch out for him."

"I'll do what I can," the rogue replied, "but I'm not making any promises."

Vadania stepped forward and said, "Meet us outside the city. Mialee and I will get Malthooz to safety. Look for us to the east of the main road."

Mialee poked her head around the corner in time to see gnolls, scattered by Krusk's unexpected charge, milling in the street. They waited for commands that were not coming. Yauktul stood in their midst fondling Wotherwill's staff. Krusk and Lidda had smashed through the gnolls without pausing, on their way to the guild hall.

"We should move," she said, stepping back around the building and dropping down next to Vadania. "We can't do anything for them, but we might still save Malthooz."

The druid nodded in silent agreement.

Each of them took one of the half-orc's arms, and they

raised him from the ground. Mialee staggered under the load, trying to keep weight off her own injured knee. Struggling and stumbling, they started moving slowly toward the edge of the city.

"The roads will be guarded," Vadania said. "They might not be looking for us specifically, but we're not the most inconspicuous or innocent-looking group right now."

"The docks," Malthooz wheezed. "I know a way."

Vadania looked at Mialee and the wizard shrugged.

"Trust me," Malthooz said. "We can use a boat. Lidda and I saw it earlier."

The wizard smiled. It was a good idea. She looked at the druid.

"Krusk and Lidda are expecting us inland, to the east, along the main road."

"Don't worry about Krusk," Mialee replied. "He'll wait for us. He'll wait a week, or a month if he has to. He said he'd be there, and he will."

Vadania nodded, then to Malthooz she said, "Point the way."

The light of the sun was already brightening the edges of the horizon. Even that faint light, reflecting off the snow, brought crisp detail to their surroundings. Shadows sharpened and peaks of roofs were outlined in icy sparkles. The wizard wasn't sure what the gnolls were up to, but she expected that, between the staff's magic and Krusk's assault, they were no longer much of a threat to anyone but themselves.

A door opened along the side of the street, causing Mialee's heart to skip. She started to pull Malthooz to the side, hoping to get out of sight, but the face that peered at them in the dim light pulled back as quickly as it emerged. The startled stranger obviously recognized their battered forms as the approach of trouble and thought better of getting mixed up with them.

We must look awful, Mialee thought.

She tried to imagine what must be going through that

person's head. At first it made her smile, but the smile faded with the thought that she was stuck in the middle of the situation.

"We won't be so lucky when the whole city comes alive," Vadania said.

She pulled ahead, pushing them to move faster.

"That will be any minute by the look of it," Mialee replied.

As they rounded the next block, Mialee saw the top of a mast showing above the roof of a squat warehouse. The docks were just beyond the next lane. The ship's sail was bunched under a spar, its folds catching the full light of the sun as it broke the horizon.

Any minute now, the wizard told herself, and the city will be awake.

They passed the next row of buildings and moved along the ranks of ships that lined the harbor front. There, at least, two oddly-dressed people helping a stumbling friend wouldn't attract much attention.

"It's not far," Malthooz said, "beyond the next pier."

Mialee could feel the half-orc's strength giving way. His weight on her shoulder was increasing and his steps growing more unsteady. Whenever he faltered, his bulk threatened to drag her to the ground.

Just a bit more, Mialee told herself, praying that he could hang on and stay conscious until they reached their destination.

Malthooz whispered, "Stop."

Lifting his shaking hand, he pointed to the top of a ladder that showed just above the edge of the dock. They moved over to it and Vadania scrambled down. She stopped halfway and shifted to the side, hooking one leg around the ladder to brace herself. Mialee helped Malthooz get his foot on the top rung.

An arrow whistled past the wizard's ear. The gnolls were advancing down the row of ships. At their head was the pack-master, urging them on while holding Wotherwill's staff high above his head.

"Gnolls! Hurry," Mialee cursed as she watched Malthooz drop from sight.

How he found the strength to cling to the ladder, she didn't know. She leaped down, bypassing the ladder entirely, to land on a heap of rope on the lower dock. Despite Vadania's help, Malthooz lost his grip and the two of them crashed down as well.

The three of them struggled back to their feet and stumbled, dragged, and pushed themselves to the end of the dock, where a ship's boat was tied up. Vadania jumped in, then cushioned the fall of the half-orc when Mialee pushed him over the edge of the dock. Water sloshed into the small craft as they tumbled against the gunwale.

Arrows flew overhead and thunked against the sides of the boat or skipped erratically off the dock. The gnoll leader stood at the top of the ladder, waving the staff. His troops milled to either side of him, disorganized and disoriented but still dangerous. Spittle flew from the commander's snout as he barked and shouted at his pack. His words were incoherent, but the gnolls needed no encouragement to keep firing on the rowboat.

"If you have any ideas at all, do something quick," urged Vadania.

Mialee heard the druid's words, but only as background noise. Her fingers were already rummaging through the pouch at her belt with practiced familiarity. Vials and coins were hastily pushed aside or flipped out onto the bottom of the boat until she found what she was after. Mialee's hand brush something smooth and cold, and her fingers snapped around it. She yanked the bone scroll case from the bag and struck it against the side of the boat. The case split into pieces, letting the scroll spill into the wizard's waiting hands.

With the scroll clutched tightly, Mialee dropped to the bottom of the boat and rolled onto her back next to Malthooz.

She ignored the arrows flying overhead, and the howls of the gnolls who thought they'd shot her, and she started reading from the scroll.

The magic tingled as it welled up in her hands. The words on the scroll twisted, blurred, and flowed together. She repeated the words seven times as the spidery, magical script faded from the face of the parchment. Fire coursed through the elf's veins as she raised herself up and stretched her arms toward the clustered gnolls. The used scroll fluttered into the harbor, sending out a series of concentric ripples as it settled on the surface of the water.

A spot of fire appeared in the air at the edge of the wizard's hand, looking like the pea-sized light of a firefly. The luminescent bauble streaked up the length of the dock and struck the pack-master in the chest.

The gnoll commander stared in wonder at the tiny light, unsure whether it was getting closer, or moving at all. As it hit him, his eyes grew wide with comprehension. A slight tremor ran through the air when light and leather met. The bead of magic drew oxygen in around itself, then let go. Fire and heat erupted into a blazing sphere of destruction.

Howls from the dying creatures could be heard above the whoosh and hum of the ball of fire. The cloud of flame engulfed the row of gnolls. Mialee flew back against the side of the boat as a wave of heat and flame passed overhead. She smelled the pungent stink of her own burning hair, singed by the searing graze of the flames. The scene at the end of the dock wavered through blurring and distorting lines of heat.

In the space of a few breaths, the pack was reduced to twisted, ashen shapes on the scorched planks. Their charred remains smoldered and crackled. Small piles of melted, misshapen arrowheads marked where quivers of arrows had burned away. Small embers still glowed, showing dots of red light along the length of the wharf. The tar-soaked timbers kept them alive, feeding them with a steady trickle of fuel.

Mialee pushed herself to her feet. She climbed out of the boat and stumbled down the dock, tripping over an embedded arrow.

The smell from the gnoll commander's body was overpowering. Mialee held her hands across her nose as she rolled the blackened corpse over with the toe of her boot. Wotherwill's staff was still clutched in the creature's skeletal hand. As she took hold of the artifact, the bones of the gnoll's fingers disintegrated. A quick shove with her heel sent the foul corpse tumbling into the bay. It sank slowly, leaving behind a sooty slick.

Vadania called to Mialee from the rowboat.

The wizard looked around and saw that the dock was rapidly coming to life and moving in her direction. She sliced the rope holding the craft to its mooring, hopped in, and used the staff to shove off from the dock. Vadania already had the oars slipped into the locks, and the two of them worked together to maneuver the boat out across the harbor. Mialee put her aching back into the work, watching the staff roll from side to side across the bottom of the boat.

Lidda stepped around the corner in time to see the barbarian crash headlong into the ranks of the gnolls. Those in his path were bowled to the ground and the rest scattered in all directions, trying to get beyond the reach of his sweeping axe.

She moved in the half-orc's wake, using the uproar and the darkness to hide her passage. The confused gnolls were too concerned about the possibility of Krusk turning back and charging them again to be aware of the small shape passing by in the shadows. Slowly, Yauktul pushed them back into a pack and they started moving again, toward Vadania, Mialee, and Malthooz. They weren't moving fast, the rogue noted, least of all Yauktul. The leader of the pack muttered to himself under his breath as though he was engaged in an argument with someone unseen. His jaw snapped from side to side as he engaged himself in dialogue. Lidda was not sure who was winning the debate, but she had no time to find out. Farther ahead, she saw Krusk jog to the far end of the alley and disappear around a corner.

The others would have to deal with the gnolls, Lidda decided, and she sprinted off in pursuit of the half-orc. They hadn't noticed her passing. She hoped the others would be as lucky.

The rogue rounded the bend at the end of the alley only to see Krusk turning down another street. At each corner it was the same. The barbarian wasn't pushing himself, but his legs were much longer than the halfling's. It was all Lidda could do to keep track of his twistings and turnings. She knew that even if she lost sight of Krusk, she could follow him by the heavy boot prints he left behind on the snow-dusted road and by the spatterings of red blood that also marked the trail. Clearly, at least some of the blood on his armor was his own. He probably didn't even know he was bleeding, Lidda thought, or if he did, he didn't care. He would not stop until either he or Flint was dead.

Lidda pushed herself harder, hoping to catch up to her quarry. Storefronts and inns raced past. From out of nowhere, a stooped form materialized directly in the rogue's path. With a yelp, Lidda slammed into the man. The two of them tumbled to the ground in a tangle of arms and legs. Lidda felt the chill of slush oozing across her chest as they slid to a stop. She lifted her head and saw Krusk receding into the distance. At her side, the man cursed her, shaking his fist. She jumped to her feet in one swift movement and ran on, but she took a different turn than the one Krusk had taken.

Lidda had little doubt where the barbarian was heading, even though he seemed uncertain of the route. There was a quicker way to the thieves guild, and the halfling intended to take it. Either Flint was weaving through the streets trying to shake Krusk's trail, Lidda thought, or the barbarian had already lost it and was desperately looking for the guild himself. Either way, the rogue knew that she could get there ahead of him. She cut across a wide junction of streets and passed into an alleyway. If she was wrong, Krusk would pay the price, but she would never catch up to him the way he was moving.

More of the city was stirring now that the sun was lifting the morning chill. People were entering the streets all around Lidda. Merchants and mongers, the city's earliest risers, were hurrying to the market, hoping to beat their competitors to the choicest stalls. None of them paid any attention to the rogue as she sped past, and she was thankful that their own pressing business kept the peddlers from noticing her. She doubted that the wounded and raging barbarian would be so easy to ignore, and he wouldn't allow himself to be delayed. She brushed by a man pulling a cart loaded with pots and pans and came around the corner of the street that fronted the guild. The din of the copper wares trundling over the rough cobbles rattled behind her.

Krusk was approaching from the other direction. The barbarian looked horrible, like a figure from a nightmare. His gait was strong, but his gashed and spattered armor was shiny with frozen blood. Crimson streaked his face and outlined his eyes. A thin layer of reddened frost glistened on the razor edge of his axe. Lidda dashed in front of him as he jogged up the stairs in front of the guild house. She caught his elbow as he raised the heavy axe to bash in the front door.

"Krusk," she hissed, "there's a better way."

The barbarian stopped, axe poised and said, "Flint is inside. This way's fine. "

Lidda clung to his raised arm.

"You don't have to die here, Krusk," she pleaded. "I'll get you inside a way that Flint doesn't suspect. You can take her by surprise."

Lidda grabbed the handle of Krusk's axe and slowly pulled the weapon down. The barbarian's chest heaved. Lidda saw fresh blood trickling from two gashes in his armor, one across his ribs and the other, much deeper, on his thigh.

"Just get me inside," Krusk said.

She slipped her tiny hand over the knuckles of Krusk's huge paw and pulled him away from the door, down the steps, and around the side of the building.

Eva Flint burst into her room. She moved around the side of her desk, drawing a small leather pouch from inside her cloak. Reaching under the top of the oak furniture, she manipulated a series of dials and twisted a handle to the side as the last of the trap's mechanisms were disarmed. She yanked open the drawer and started stuffing handfuls of gems into the pouch.

Outside her chamber, the guild master heard the sounds of fighting in the warehouse beyond. She kicked her chair aside and knelt on the stone floor. With a dagger, she pried up a small section of flooring, then grabbed the iron handle hidden beneath. When she pulled it, a larger section of flooring fell away, revealing a concealed chute.

Flint stuffed the sack of treasures into her cloak and dropped through the hole into the darkness beyond. The gemstones weren't much, but they would have to do. She landed in the broad, semicircular tube of the sewer system that ran under the expanse of Newcoast.

The treasure would at least get her to the next city.

A man came at Krusk waving a crowbar. He should have known better. The barbarian's axe whistled under the clumsy weapon and sliced into the man's side. He hit the floor before the crowbar did.

Lidda was right behind the half-orc, reloading her crossbow, watching as her own target fell to the floor with a bolt buried in his chest. She scanned the cavernous room for more assailants, but nothing moved except her and Krusk. They were in the guild's main warehouse. It was a massive room for holding goods, both legitimate and not, that passed through Flint's hands on their way to various and sometimes questionable clients.

Behind the pair of companions lay a trail of bodies. Poor fools, Lidda thought. They had no idea why they died. Most of them were probably no more than laborers, simple men who kept up the appearance that the place was a shipping business. Some, though, were undoubtedly hopeful thieves, performing minor tasks for Flint and waiting for the guild master to grant them favor. They paid the price for their ambition on the edge of Krusk's axe and across the sights of her crossbow. Lidda knew that little separated her from these men except luck. Unlike them, however, she had it and they didn't. She would not die as a pawn in one of Flint's games of trickery.

Lidda looked up as she heard the crunch of Krusk's boot breaking through the wooden door to Flint's chambers. The rogue followed the barbarian into the woman's office, entering just as Krusk's head disappeared through a hole in the floor behind Flint's desk.

Lidda's boots landed in ankle-deep muck. Just ahead of Krusk, she saw Flint dashing away through the dappled light that filtered into the area from gutters in the street above. The sewers of Newcoast mirrored the city's streets, catching the runoff and sewage and carrying it to the harbor. Anyone who knew the streets could navigate the sewers.

The halfling splashed along behind the barbarian. She watched in dismay as Krusk raced ahead, and she knew from her earlier experience that she couldn't keep up. Krusk was driven by passion and rage. Even so, Lidda doubted that he could overtake the guild master, who was unwounded.

Lidda dropped to her knee in the thick water. The stench of the sewer clouded her head in a way that felt almost as foul as the waste soaking into her boots and leggings. This stretch of sewer was long and straight, and Lidda could dimly make out the guild master ahead. She lined up Eva in her sights, weaving slightly with the woman's motion, keeping one eye on Krusk as he bobbed back and forth across her line of fire.

Lidda knew that she was taking a long chance. She couldn't risk hitting Krusk, even if that meant letting Flint escape. This was the only shot she would get.

Flint turned to head down a side tunnel. For one moment, that turn carried her clear of Krusk and gave Lidda a clean shot. She squeezed the trigger.

The bolt darted from the crossbow, whistled past Krusk, and nailed Flint in the hip. The guild master tumbled head over heels, her scream echoing through the tunnels.

When Krusk barged around the corner, he was startled to find the woman on her feet, wide-stanced, facing him with weapons drawn.

Krusk slammed into her like a runaway barrel. The two of them went down with a splash into the sewage. The barbarian lost his grip on his axe and it clattered against the tunnel wall. He scrambled toward it, but Flint was just a bit quicker. Her sword bit across his shoulder, but the rushed attack was badly aimed and caused little injury. Still, she was between Krusk and his weapon. He rolled away from the steel blade and jumped to his feet at the side of the tunnel.

Flint placed her boot on Krusk's axe. There was no teasing smile on her face now.

"You've cost me everything, half-breed," she snarled. "Prepare yourself for whatever hell is reserved for barbarians. Your time here is up."

Krusk laughed at her.

"You know nothing about hell," he said, "but you will. It's you who have no time left."

Krusk made a snapping move toward the woman. Flint swung her sword menacingly in that direction, keeping him from getting close. Krusk circled, trying to get closer to his axe, but Flint moved with him, and the tunnel was too narrow for a wide maneuver.

"I don't care whether I cut off your head with my axe or crush your neck with my hands, thief," Krusk growled. "Do you?"

Lidda peered around the corner. She leveled the crossbow down the tunnel, but the weaving fighters left her no clear shot.

"Damn it, Krusk," she cursed, "get out of the way and I'll finish this now!"

"She's mine," Krusk growled, deliberately stepping in Lidda's way.

Flint lunged with lightning quickness. The half-orc jumped back, narrowly avoiding the tip of the sword that danced in front of his face.

"Forgive me, Krusk," Lidda whispered.

She stepped behind the barbarian and kicked at the back of his knee. Already unbalanced by his leap away from Flint's sword, Krusk's legs buckled and he toppled backward to the tunnel floor.

Lidda was already rolling to the side, away from Krusk's tumble. She caught Flint in her sight and fired. The string on her crossbow hummed as it sent a bolt hurtling toward the woman. The tip struck her square in the chest and passed completely through her body. Seconds later, Lidda heard it splash far down the tunnel.

The guild master stumbled sideways against the wall. Her sword arm drooped and the weapon fell, disappearing into the brown water. Flint struggled for breath. Red bubbles grew and burst around the hole in the front of her armor each time she inhaled. She groaned, but stayed on her feet. Her right hand fumbled for the dagger at her belt while with her left hand she painfully stuffed a kerchief into the hole in her chest.

Krusk roared and jumped back to his feet.

"She was mine!" he snarled through bared fangs.

His fist was raised against Lidda.

A splash followed by a sputtering laugh interrupted him. Flint had slumped to the floor, but she was sitting up against the wall. Blood flecked her lips as she spoke.

"She killed me, barbarian," Flint laughed. "The half-pint beat the half-breed." A cough brought bloody foam rolling down her chin. "But that's not the funny part," she continued. "Do you think my death will save you? Now you have even more murders on your heads. Both the city and the guild will be hot for your blood."

Flint's breath came in short, gurgling gasps. She wiped the blood from her mouth.

"I'm glad your friend died. Or was he your brother?"

The barbarian moved to strike the woman but his fist was stopped by Lidda's hand on his shoulder.

"Just leave her to die, Krusk," she said.

Flint smiled again, reveling in Krusk's pain. She turned to Lidda.

"Things turned out poorly for you, too, little one," she said. "You crossed a guild . . . who will take you in now . . . ?"

Her words trailed off, but her eyes danced with a wicked light.

Krusk stooped and took the dagger from her hand, then he crouched over Flint's body. Lidda's view of Flint was momentarily blocked, and Lidda was glad. When the barbarian turned around again, he held Flint's dripping head in his left hand. His right, holding the knife, glistened with bright blood. He tossed the knife away carelessly and retrieved his axe.

"Now we both killed her," the barbarian said.

Lidda had no reply to that.

"Let's move," she said. "Malthooz and the others still need us. We don't have much time, if any, before last night's activities are discovered."

The rogue's ribs were throbbing, but she took Krusk by his knotted, blood-stained fingers and the two of them made their way down the tunnel.

"There's light ahead," Krusk said, motioning with his grisly trophy.

The glow came from around a corner ahead of them. Lidda nodded. She could smell the salt of the harbor. As they rounded the bend, she saw the iron bars of a grating, and just beyond the bars, the light of morning was rippling atop the surface of the bay.

Krusk set down the head and grabbed the bars. They weren't meant to keep people in, so he had little difficulty bending two of them apart. He opened them just enough to squeeze himself through, then, pausing only to pick up Flint's head and without so much as a glance to where he was going to land, he stepped through.

Lidda followed behind him. The freezing water of the harbor took her breath away, but it was at least clean.

The druid saw her companions splash into the water near the piers. She pulled hard on an oar, spinning the rowboat around. Malthooz lay in the bow of the craft, his head cradled in the folds of Mialee's robe. Vadania knew that he didn't have much time left. She'd been holding them in the shadow of the cliffs, but that offered only limited safety. She hadn't expected to see them plunge out of a sewer tunnel, then again, she hadn't really expected to see them again at all.

Fire raced along the docks, backlighting Vadania as she laid her back into the oars. The spreading flames from Mialee's fireball had ignited one of the neighboring ships. In no time, the whole area was in chaos as captains and crew struggled to get their vessels away from the advancing flames. A thick black cloud hung in the air above the city. The inferno fed on tar-soaked planks and pilings.

"What have we done?" the druid muttered to herself.

"Only what we had to do," Mialee responded behind her.

The staff still rested in the bottom of the boat. Vadania kicked it and the thing rolled to the stern. The druid shuddered as she thought about what it might have done in the wrong hands, what it might still do. She'd already seen enough of the artifact's twisted magic, and she suspected that was only a hint of its real power.

By the time they reached the rogue and the barbarian, the two were at the end of their endurance. The icy water had reduced them to simply struggling against the weight of their armor and weapons in an effort to keep their heads above water. Lidda's lips were blue, her skin pale white from the frigid chill of the harbor. Even Krusk's normal gray complexion looked waxy and pale.

Mialee hauled the halfling woman into the rowboat and set her down near Malthooz, but between herself and the druid, they could not get Krusk over the side without threatening to upend the craft and dump them all into the bay. The shivering half-orc simply clung to the transom as Vadania rowed for the far shore.

"Flint's dead," Lidda said through chattering teeth.

Vadania glanced at the frozen head, still clutched tightly in Krusk's hand and bouncing against the gunwale. The news was no surprise. She nodded grimly.

The port of Newcoast still burned. No boats followed in the company's wake. Ships milled in the harbor or headed toward the open sea, but none seemed to pay any special attention to them.

At last, the bow ground up on the gravel along the southern shore of the harbor.

"It will take a while for the news of our escape to spread through all this confusion," Mialee said as she stepped out of the vessel and struggled to drag it farther up the beach. "That's if it ever does."

"I guess that depends on how deep the lines of deception run," the druid replied. "Who knows what and who cares?"

Mialee and Vadania helped the halfling to her feet, and the

three of them carried Malthooz to dry land. Krusk, shivering and stiff, waded in and collapsed beside them.

Malthooz opened his eyes as the four of them hovered over him. He smiled when he looked at Lidda and Krusk.

"I knew that you'd make it," he said as his eyes fell on the symbol of Pelor around Krusk's neck.

Krusk fingered the wooden disc. He lifted it over his head and set it down on Malthooz's chest.

"I brought you this, too," he said, swinging the guild master's severed head before Malthooz's wide eyes.

"That's a fine gift," Malthooz whispered.

"You grab his legs," the barbarian said to Vadania and Mialee as he slipped his arms under Malthooz's shoulders.

A word from Malthooz stopped him.

"Leave me be, Krusk. I will go no farther today."

Vadania looked around them. Farther up the slope were the edges of pastures and farm fields. A man stood there, watching the port burn. He glanced at the companions then went back to his work, unloading bales of hay from a rickety wooden cart for the flock of sheep that hovered in the meadow around him.

Malthooz beckoned Krusk with his finger to come closer. The barbarian knelt close to his friend's face, his ear hovering just over the half-orc's mouth. A few words passed between the two of them, but none of the others could hear what was said. Vadania turned away. It wasn't her business.

Krusk stood up and moved away. Vadania and the other women watched as Malthooz's head sank back down to the ground. A smile spread across his lips as his gaze fell on the head, and a look of serenity came over his brow. Then, with a rasping sigh, he was gone.

Epilogue . . . The companions hustled away from New-coast as the ocean was blazing with the orange light of the setting sun. Black smoke still obscured the eastern sky. It hung like a blanket in the thin, still air. She was glad that the whole place hadn't gone up in flames. She turned onto the trail that led to the Deepwood with the rest of her companions, the weight of Wotherwill's staff bouncing in the center of her shoulder blades.

None of them had any way of knowing how long it would be before the evidence of their fight with Flint and her forces would lead to their pursuit, or if it ever would. They had even less of an idea who might take up their trail. Corruption ran to the highest levels and the deepest coffers of the city government; that much was more than apparent. Between the city authorities and the guild, the only thing that would be certain was mistrust.

It was assumed that they had no allies at this point, no one to turn to if they were caught. None of them were eager to protest their innocence. They wanted to place as much distance between themselves and Newcoast as they could.

They made no attempt to conceal their passage. Distance, not stealth, seemed their best friend. They wound their way, in the early evening hours, across the rolling farmlands and into the edge of Deepwood.

Krusk carried Malthooz's shrouded body on a makeshift litter that he dragged behind himself. He showed little emotion. Vadania knew that he mourned in his own way. The druid studied Krusk as he trudged along. He wore the symbol of Pelor around his neck again, even though Vadania knew that Krusk had no interest in converting. She didn't know whether the wooden trinket eased his pain, or if he saw it as a talisman against evil spirits. The others left the barbarian alone in his silence, each of them dealing with their friend's passing in their own private way.

They traveled for three days, back to the beach where the splintered remains of *Treachery* still rested half-buried on the beach. Bits of the hull littered the high water mark, heavy and swollen with sea water, almost indistinguishable from other, unrelated pieces of driftwood. Most of the vessel remained in place—a little more battered, a little more deeply settled in the shifting sand.

Krusk set to work immediately. He attacked the wreckage with his axe, taking revenge on it for all the unresolved wrongs of the previous weeks. When he had finally swung his arms to exhaustion, he gathered the timbers and piled them on the sand. With rope from the fallen rigging, he crafted a makeshift raft in the dying hours of the day.

Vadania and the other women watched the barbarian tie the last knot on his raft, then they helped him carry the wrapped form of Malthooz to it as the tide peaked around its forward edge. Krusk wedged the tattered head of the guild master under Malthooz's feet. He started to lift the symbol of Pelor from his chest but let it fall back again. Instead, he turned away and fetched a burning brand from the fire.

As he returned to the raft with the torch, Krusk saw Vadania adding something else next to Flint's head—Wotherwill's staff.

Krusk growled, "That thing is a desecration. Take it away."

Vadania stood her ground, so Krusk stepped forward and reached for the staff.

"Leave it, Krusk," Vadania commanded, and she stepped in his way. "This isn't only about you. It's for all of us."

Krusk's eyes narrowed on the druid's face. His hand tightened into a fist. Seeing it, Mialee and Lidda rushed to the druid's side.

"Don't do this, Krusk," Lidda hissed.

The rogue folded her arms across her chest and stood next to Vadania. Mialee stood to the druid's other side. Together, the three women formed a wall against the barbarian.

The druid held out her hand, but Krusk shook his massive head. Vadania stepped forward and lifted the symbol of Pelor from around Krusk's neck. She wrapped the cord of the trinket around the wizard's staff.

"This is how it must be," she said, backing away from the raft.

Still scowling, Krusk stepped forward with the burning brand thrust ahead. The flame sputtered weakly in the sea breeze. Vadania reached out her hand and placed it on the torch, just ahead of Krusk's. She intoned an arcane phrase and the small yellow flame grew into a white blaze. Together they touched it to the planks and the flames raced across the raft. With a mighty shove, Krusk pushed the mass of wood into the receding tide.

They watched in silence as the blazing raft floated out on the waves. The orange flames that engulfed it melted into the reds and pinks of the sunset. Eventually the flames and the sea met in a confrontation of steam and smoke, and the remnants of the raft swirled from their view.

None of them said a thing as they returned to their tiny campfire. One by one, the women curled into their blankets and fell to sleep.

Krusk stayed up longer, gazing into the fire and reflecting on the events of the past few weeks. Finally, in the early hours of the morning, he rose and opened his own bedroll, but he didn't lie down. Instead he withdrew a slender wooden club, the one he'd fashioned for Malthooz. He held it for a while, remembering another night when he sat up late by a fire, making the weapon.

Krusk turned and set the club on the waning coals. He watched until the embers ignited the weapon. It flared brightly, sending tiny tongues of flame and glowing sparks upward into the dark sky, but it quickly burned down into a flickering line, then crumbled among the embers.

Capture the thrill of D&D® adventuring!

These six new titles from T.H. Lain put you
in the midst of the heroic party as it encounters
deadly magic, sinister plots, and fearsome creatures.
Join the adventure!

THE BLOODY EYE

TREACHERY'S WAKE

PLAGUE OF ICE
May 2003

THE SUNDERED ARMS
July 2003

RETURN OF THE DAMNED
October 2003

THE DEATH RAY
December 2003

The Avatar Series

New editions of the event that changed all Faerûn…and the gods that ruled it.

SHADOWDALE
Book 1 • *Scott Ciencin*

The gods have been banished to the surface of Faerûn,
and magic runs mad throughout the land.

May 2003

TANTRAS
Book 2 • *Scott Ciencin*

Bane and his ally Myrkul, god of Death, set in motion a plot to seize
Midnight and the Tablets of Fate for themselves.

June 2003

The New York Times *best-seller!*
WATERDEEP
Book 3 • *Troy Denning*

Midnight and her companions must complete their quest by traveling
to Waterdeep. But Cyric and Myrkul are hot on their trail.

July 2003

PRINCE OF LIES
Book 4 • *James Lowder*

Cyric, now god of Strife, wants revenge on Mystra, goddess of Magic.

September 2003

CRUCIBLE: THE TRIAL OF CYRIC THE MAD
Book 5 • *Troy Denning*

The other gods have witnessed Cyric's madness
and are determined to overthrow him.

October 2003

Starlight & Shadows

New York Times best-selling author Elaine
Cunningham finally completes this stirring trilogy
of dark elf Liriel Baenre's travels across Faerûn!
All three titles feature stunning art from award-
winning fantasy artist Todd Lockwood.

New paperback editions!

DAUGHTER OF THE DROW
Book 1

Liriel Baenre, a free-spirited drow princess, ventures beyond the dark halls
of Menzoberranzan into the upper world. There, in the world of light, she
finds friendship, magic, and battles that will test her body and soul.

February 2003

TANGLED WEBS
Book 2

Liriel and Fyodor, her barbarian companion, walk the twisting streets of
Skullport in search of adventure. But the dark hands of Liriel's past still
reach out to clutch her and drag her back to the Underdark.

March 2003

New in hardcover – the long-awaited finale!

WINDWALKER
Book 3

Their quest complete, Liriel and Fyodor set out for the barbarian's homeland
to return the magical Windwalker amulet. Amid the witches of Rashemen,
Liriel learns of new magic and love and finds danger everywhere.

April 2003

The War of Souls ends now.

The New York Times best-seller from
DRAGONLANCE® co-creators

Margaret Weis & Tracy Hickman

available for the first time in paperback!

The stirring conclusion to the epic trilogy

DRAGONS OF A VANISHED MOON
The War of Souls, Volume III

A small band of heroes, led by an incorrigible kender, prepares to battle
an army of the dead led by a seemingly invincible female warrior. A dragon
overlord provides a glimmer of hope to those who fight the darkness, but
true victory—or utter defeat—lies in the secret of time's riddles.

March 2003

Legend of the Five Rings.

The Four Winds Saga

Only one can claim the Throne of Rokugan.

WIND OF JUSTICE
Third Scroll
Rich Wulf

Naseru, the most cold-hearted and scheming of the royal heirs, will stop at nothing to sit upon the Throne of Rokugan. But when dark forces in the City of Night threaten his beloved Empire, Naseru must learn to wield the most unlikely weapon of all — justice.

June 2003

WIND OF TRUTH
Fourth Scroll
Ree Soesbee

Sezaru, one of the most powerful wielders of magic in all Rokugan, has never desired his father's throne, but destiny calls to the son of Toturi. Here, in the final volume of the Four Winds Saga, all will be decided.

December 2003

Now available:

THE STEEL THRONE
Prelude
Edward Bolme

WIND OF HONOR
First Scroll
Ree Soesbee

WIND OF WAR
Second Scroll
Jess Lebow